MAY   2021

SWITCH

SW/TCH

by **A.S. King**

DUTTON BOOKS

DUTTON BOOKS

An imprint of Penguin Random House LLC, New York

First published in the United States of America by Dutton Books,
an imprint of Penguin Random House LLC, 2021

Visit us online at penguinrandomhouse.com.

Library of Congress Cataloging-in-Publication Data is available.

Printed in the United States of America
ISBN 9780525555513
10   9   8   7   6   5   4   3   2   1

Design by Anna Booth
Text set in Joanna MT Std

For the class of 2020

Time is the most unknown of all unknown things.

—Aristotle

Any man can call time out, but no man can say how long the time out will be.

—Kurt Vonnegut Jr.

Knock hard. Life is deaf.

—Mimi Parent

SWITCH

Prologue I / Time Stopped

THE FOLD

We have arrived at a fold in time and space. Nothing moves forward. A scientific dilemma yet to be solved fully.

You are probably confused.

We are confused, too.

Analog, digital, stopwatches—cell phone providers argued over the idea of fake time / decided it would be unethical / left us with our lock-screen picture—no clock / no date.

It is, and has been, June 23, 2020, for nine months now.

It's a fluke. An irregularity in space. We just have to be patient. Our hair grows / babies are born / people die. But time has stopped. We are being held for ransom / no one knows what the ransom is / who to give it to.

SOLUTION TIME

By the Fourth of July, things disappeared from grocery shelves / people hoarded everything from yeast to taco shells / couldn't stop watching the news. Supermarkets put limits on milk and meat, and only 25 percent had toilet paper, sometimes guarded by signs about how God was watching so people didn't buy too much.

Inside of a month, the secretary of education enacted "Solution Time." Curricula crafted for every classroom / every school / university / every state, to solve the world's time problem. Students would figure it out / be sufficiently distracted.

The first outcome of Solution Time was N3WCLOCK, invented

by three nineteen-year-olds in a summer-session community college classroom in Reading, Pennsylvania.

N3WCLOCK exists in one place—N3WCLOCK.com—on the internet. It is now the most-visited web page of all time. It tells you what time and date it would be if Earth hadn't fallen into a fold in time and space. For the record, N3WCLOCK says it's presently Monday, March 15, 2021, 16:11. They use military time just in case this is really an alien invasion.

By August, politicians had decided to rely on N3WCLOCK worldwide, and everything returned to normal. Back-to-school sales drove record-high profits. Our clocks stood still. Our egg timers never dinged. Yet we were on time for dentist appointments and we didn't burn dinner.

YOU GET USED TO IT

That's what they said would happen. Sun still rises in the morning / sets in the evening. We still eat dinner at around 18:00.

I refuse to pretend that N3WCLOCK is the solution to being in a fold in time and space, though. Solution Time was not invented so we could find new ways to lie to ourselves.

I'm looking for the Real Solution.

I think it has something to do with giving a shit about people.

THE SWITCH

In the center of our house, there is a switch. It's like a light switch—on the wall in the hallway outside the kitchen. No one knows what the switch controls, and no one wants to know. So no one in my family ever touches it. And we don't take any visitors.

This one day, Daddy built a box around the switch as a safety. When he did that, I wanted to find out everything about that switch. I pried off the box. I stared at the workings / chewed them like gum / but was too scared to flip it / blow the bubble.

Nailed the box back on. Ignored the box. Spited the box. Until Daddy built another box—a bigger one / plywood / to contain both the switch and the first box.

This went on for two years. Bigger and bigger boxes. To keep us safe.

I have been nailed into box #7. My sister in #9, my brother in #11. Daddy lives outside the boxes, hammering.

NOT WHAT YOU THINK

Daddy is from Somewhere Else. A place where things are different and where people are secure. He is a naturalized citizen, but there's nothing natural about being American, he says. All slick talk and bullshit, he says. Daddy comes from a place where every word is honest / nobody shoots you.

This place is war / he is a soldier with six-inch steel nails. This is a circus and he is juggling all of us. War juggling / weapons in flight. Circuits in circles. Me, Richard, sister. Me, Richard, sister.

I am a missile launcher.

Richard is a rifle.

Sister is an assortment of bombs.

Part One:
AFT3RMATH

The Paleolithic

BOX #7

Box #7 makes no sense. It's supposed to contain me but there's a hole. A me-shaped hole. When I slide through it, I find the entire world. I slide through it every so-called weekday morning—and go to the high school.

My brother Richard is presently in his box. #11. No him-shaped hole. If he wants to go anywhere—like classes for his sophomore year at community college—he has to use the front door or climb out a window.

Sometimes I hear him crying in there. Sometimes I hear him skipping rope so fast I can feel the wind of it. Sometimes I hear him practicing Portuguese. I asked him one time why he's learning Portuguese. He said, "So I can talk to myself and none of you will know what I'm saying."

Richard found high school to be educational. He learned how to be a rifle there. Load him and squeeze the trigger—ideas come out / clubs get formed / find yourself singing holiday songs at the old-folks home or picking up trash on the side of a highway.

But Richard / Rifle has no bayonet. He cannot stab ideas, he can only shoot them.

The only thing educational to me in high school so far is the wide selection of javelins in the track and field shed. I stab ideas with them. They teach me how to fly through time when no time exists.

TRACK / FIELD

When I was born, I did not know how to throw a javelin. I am now sixteen and I know this: either you are on the oval / track, or inside the oval / field.

   I.   am inside the oval
   II. am the jav as it flies overhead
   III. missile seeking its target

Until three weeks ago, I didn't know about track and field. It's a freak accident no one knew was coming. My arm has something in it. My body has a need to propel. There is gunpowder behind it / kapow / I am downright Olympic.

It was a natural progression. I wasn't supposed to be in that particular gym class, but our schedules changed to allow Solution Time and I accidentally skipped a PE credit / Tru Becker please report to the guidance office.

It was way too cold to be going outside for Intro to Track & Field because it was the first week of pretend-March, but it was refreshing, too. I didn't have any choice, and this is what Daddy always said: Find reason to like the thing you must do. It makes easier.

I didn't need to find a reason / the reason was clear. I was in the AFT3RMATH / sister had moved away—I could be good at Intro to Track & Field because for the first time in my life, no one was waiting at home to make fun of me / make me pay for being good at Intro to Track & Field. Daddy, Richard, and I were the only ones left and Daddy was busy with the boxes / Richard was busy being a good boy / rifle at community college. I could do anything I wanted to and do it well. This was a novelty / a dare.

I was okay at short running. Decent at jumping once I got my footing. But then I threw a javelin for the first time.

"Holy shit!" I heard Coach Turner say.

The first time I watched it fly, I was part of it. Even in the spring morning grass / shoes weighted down with damp, I was flying.

We watched it / me land far away from the other students' attempts / stabbing the idea of failure.

"Becker!" he yelled as he jogged toward me. "How'd you know how to do that?"

I shrugged.

"You threw one of these before, right?" he asked.

"Can I throw another one?"

He gave me another javelin. I rolled my neck and shoulders, weighed it in my hand to feel the balance, then took three sideways steps, bounced, and tossed it again. I felt my arm still part of it, pull me off the ground and behind it. I felt sixty-miles-per-hour.

Gym class had never been interesting before.

Coach Turner sat me down later that day with two other track coaches and I didn't understand anything he said. Something about preseason. Something about being late. Something about missing "conditioning time." He tripped over his words while the other two coaches looked less than enthused. The only thing Coach Aimee said was "You have to maintain a B average to compete. You're going to have to bring your grades up."

When I had Daddy sign the permission slip, I didn't even know what a track team really was. I've been going to practice for two weeks now. I'm still not entirely sure.

I just know the javelins are educational every single day / taught me that none of us know what we have inside of us until it shows itself / until we take the dare.

GREEK GODDESS / SPEAR

I do not listen in class / have trouble caring about things that don't interest me. I don't know two-thirds of the elements of the periodic table or how to find x when y equals five.

I mostly read articles about psychology.

x equals why my brother Richard cries.
x equals why gym class is suddenly interesting.

I have finally found a place for myself in high school / I am here to throw a spear. Next pretend-Tuesday is our opening home meet. Carrie says away meets are the best because sometimes we don't get home until after dark and we sing on the bus.

Carrie calls me *goddess*, like this shit is Greek. But I'm Paleolithic. It's survival, not competition. When I sleep I can feel the cave around me. The predators. The danger of being good at something.

Only thing x means to me now is where it marks the spot— farther than anyone ever threw before.

Solution Time

NIGEL

Our advisor / absentee / predator for Solution Time is Nigel Andrews. Nigel is in love with himself and his Solution Time program / he invented it / it came to him in a fever dream back when Earth first landed in the fold. He is never here, even though he's supposed to be helping us complete our two Solution Time objectives.

I. Create an individual project that explores time in a new, exciting way / You will conduct this project with your group as the instructor.
II. Write a research paper about your personal solution / Your thesis statement must be clear and match your conclusion.

How anyone can find "a new, exciting way" to do anything in the same old way we do *everything* is beyond me / typical adult bullshit. Thesis / conclusion / educational missionary position. Nigel thinks "real" science is 3-D printers and advanced math / lab rats / rivalry and electric shocks. High school is precious, you know / best years of your life / why waste it on psychology.

But Nigel is also often drunk. Back in pretend-December, Len guessed from the smell of Nigel's breath. "Hard to tell on top of the Altoids, but it's presenting as gin," he said. Ellie told her dad / her dad called the school / Nigel only visits us once a month now.

I'm pretty sure Solution Time was invented as a nation-wide distraction. They schedule us to make us feel less lost / two hours every day, first thing in the morning. First quarter, we invented our research projects. Second and third quarter, we conduct our research and have team discussions about it. Fourth quarter is dedicated to writing our papers about our solutions. Our thesis statements are due in two weeks. I have no idea what mine will say.

PSYCH TEAM

We were split into groups during a day-long assembly back in pretend-September. The auditorium was its usual sea of almost all white faces / we are considered one of the "good" schools / half of us drowning in shame for it / half of us waving tiny American flags, saying we deserve the best / everything.

Our group is Psych Team: five weirdos who believe that the human mind has something to do with escaping a fold in time and space.

It only took a half hour for us to find a stack of old psychology textbooks in the back of the book closet. Nigel said that we were too far back / those books weren't for us / we'd never under-stand them. "Psychology at your age is pointless." But I walked out with a Robert Plutchik textbook and an old philosophy book, Ellie walked out with two Jean Piaget books, and Carrie picked Philip Zimbardo because the cover promised that the book would change the reader's life. Eric walked out with a Strauss and Howe about Generation X, and Len ended up with a guide for college freshman from 1958 called *Controversy* / picked it because it has a chapter in it titled "The American Sex Revolution."

The outcome of the too-far-back book-closet dive was awesome / five students with brand-new bayonets / Psych Team's projects are off the charts.

Carrie's project is about the psychology of time, focusing on Zimbardo's time perspective theory, and how each of us is affected by how we see the world and our lives through time. For example, I started out in past-negative / future-negative but I'm working toward past-positive / future-positive.

Eric's project covers epigenetics and recent discoveries that trauma passes down on a genetic level. He already has his paper mostly written: "Generation Fifteen: Dragging Fourteen Generations' Worth of Your Bullshit."

Ellie uses Jean Piaget's theory of cognitive development to explore the different results Solution Time will get from children at different stages of development. She'll then look at how those results should be shared with all age groups for further expansion. Since this would benefit Solution Time in general, Ellie's was Nigel's pet project until her dad called the school about the gin-breath.

Len wants to be a filmmaker. He records random stuff all the time and makes short documentaries. For Solution Time, he's asking us a lot of "why" questions about our futures / what are the advantages of being educated? / going to college? / what is college really for? He films parts of our conversations and will make a film of it somehow.

My Solution Time class project relies on the ideas of two dead white men.

"If everything when it occupies an equal space is at rest, and if that which is in locomotion is always occupying such a space at any moment, **the flying arrow is therefore motionless**."
— Zeno of Elea, Greek philosopher

and

"Most people think of emotions as special kinds of feelings— feelings that we describe by such words as *happy* or *sad, angry* or *jealous, or in love*. Everyone also knows that **emotions are powerful forces** influencing our behavior; people laugh, cry, become depressed, or blow up buildings under the influence of emotions."
— Robert Plutchik, American psychologist

I believe that when we are stuck in an unmoving arrow / fold in time and space, emotions are the powerful force that will break us out. Giving a shit about people isn't easy until you give a shit about yourself / secure your own oxygen mask before assisting others. Or something like that.

PLUTCHIK'S CLOCK

Zeno of Elea can be frustrating / explains my flight / gave me magic. Robert Plutchik is a lot easier to understand and is probably going to save my life.

I found him online the way people find boyfriends—before we dove into the book closet. He was a twentieth-century psychologist / invented the psychoevolutionary theory of basic emotions.

He reckoned there were eight basic emotions that could vary in intensity, and that all of them were truly primal to humans. Meaning: They aren't a choice. Meaning: They are there for a reason, just like your uvula is there so you don't spit food out your nose.

He invented an emotion wheel / a rainbow flower with eight petals. The petals have emotion-names. Joy, Trust, Fear, Surprise, Sadness, Disgust, Anger, and Anticipation. (Yellow, light green, green, blue, purple, pink, red, orange.) There's more to it than that / life-saving / Plutchik threw me an understanding of everything / myself.

I have made a Plutchik's Clock. My invention. One hand / eight stops around the rainbow flower / invented new time / Feeling Time.

With eight petals, we can go round the clock three times as opposed to the old analog / only two rotations. Every hour we can focus our feelings on to one color and we can learn about ourselves and how we navigate emotions. This is half of the magic.

The other half lives inside Zeno's arrow / like me / in flight and motionless.

The idea is that if we put ourselves in the arrow, in the here and now, we can feel what we really feel instead of pretending we don't. In my case, I will survive the AFT3RMATH by learning more about what sixteen years of living with a series of explosions did to my brain / heart / by putting my answers in a javelin and then throwing it as far as I can.

JOY

This month, pretend-March, has been my month to finish testing Plutchik's Clock on Psych Team. One hour a day / one emotion a day. We are in the kitchen area of Culinary 204, our assigned Solution Time classroom, sitting on five red stools around the faux kitchen island / dining table.

"I want to talk about Zeno again," I say.

All my teammates are mad at me for Zeno.

"Motion is not impossible. Look." Carrie waves her arms around. "I'm moving."

"But . . . you don't feel like Zeno's arrow when you triple jump?" I ask. "Like time stands still while you're in the air?"

"It goes by real fast and then there's sand up my shorts. That's about it."

I take a deep breath. "Anyway. The idea is that you have to feel your feelings in the absence of time. Remember, a lot of our emotions are complicated by time, right?"

"What day is it?" Ellie asks. "It's not Sadness again, is it? I can't do Sadness again."

"Joy."

"Oh!" she says. "I love Joy!"

We are on our third ride around Plutchik's Clock / back at the beginning. I have learned a lot about my teammates. I think the idea is gelling: Put five people in a room and make them concentrate on one emotion for an hour a day, and they can better handle that emotion going forward. This also improves their ability to give a shit about other people.

Seems obvious / not like an education, quite / probably should be.

"The couch is open. I brought yoga mats if anyone is more comfortable on the floor."

Len gets up and moves to the carpeted area of the room, unrolls a yoga mat, and sits in lotus position. Eric is already smiling with his eyes closed and his back straight at the table.

I have my Plutchik's Clock and I move its hand to the twelve o'clock position. Yellow. Joy. I open my notebook.

"What makes you feel joy?"

Carrie: Cookies!

Ellie: Nate Gardener.

Eric: Learning stuff.

Len: Jacking off to Led Zeppelin.

I write down the answers accordingly.

Carrie moves to the oven and turns it on. She removes a box of chocolate chip cookie mix from her purse, followed by an egg.

"You brought an egg?"

"Yep."

"In your purse?"

"I knew today was Joy again," she says.

While Carrie makes cookies, we write in our journals, do breathing exercises, talk, and try to put ourselves in the arrow. Eric puts on music to explain joy. It's old Cuban music because Eric says this is what his parents listen to when they make dinner. "They dance and kiss and stuff," he says. "It's pretty cool."

"My parents never kiss," Carrie says, plopping dough onto two cookie sheets.

"My dad has a new girlfriend and they can't stop touching each other," Ellie says.

"They probably have sex all the time," Len says. I've learned to not argue. It's expression for him, somehow.

"The other day they did it in the downstairs bathroom between dinner and dishes," Ellie says.

"What did you do?" I ask.

"I cleared the table with my little sister and then sat back down so I could watch them walk out of the bathroom and lie."

"Joy," I say. "Let's stay focused on joy."

Ellie says, "It makes me happy, actually, that he's happy. I mean, I wish he didn't have to divorce my mom and fuck up the whole family, but he's happier now than I ever saw him. So that matters."

Carrie says, "My parents are only married for my sake, I think."

"What gives you joy about that?" I ask.

"Stop trying to always make it come back to your clock," Carrie says. "Joy isn't everything."

"It's Joy day, Carrie." Ellie says.

"I'm making cookies. What else do you want?" She laughs, and I know that her parents are breaking up every day and trying to stay together every day, and I know someone saw her mom out at a bar in a 1990s miniskirt / too much lipstick.

THE PURPOSE

You are probably confused. You've never heard of Robert Plutchik before / don't see him in your lifeguard chair / can't see the rainbow flower. Find it / yourself in it. When there is no time, life is a treasure hunt. Even if the treasure is ugly or dirty or feels like grit in your eye. When there is no time, everything else matters.

Growth Mindset

YOUR JOB

Compete only with yourself.

The game is your life and there are no do-overs. Not even if someone has played with your life. Not even if they lit it on fire—then you are on fire and competing with yourself. Your job is to contain the flames faster than you ever have before.

Your job—resist the urge to scratch the burns.

Your job—heal.

This isn't how Coach Aimee puts it, but it's how I see it. She says things like, "You have talent and you have training. Which one is more important?" and the obvious answer, since we're about to train, is training.

The other throwers complain about the running. I don't. I like the slow laps before practice and the sprinting. It helps focus and get rid of high school bullshit. Today's high school bullshit: lunch. After Carrie bragged to the table about my whole Paleolithic thing, our friend group / Psych Team feels I will leave them behind because I will become a popular jock. I tried to convince them that I will be their friend forever. "A girl named Tru can't lie."

As I run around the track, all these things disappear.

Except *forever*. The concept is uncomfortable. I can't figure out why, as humans, we are forced to make so many forever-deals. Especially in high school. Especially while in a fold in time and space. It is the epitome of forever / the opposite of forever. It's a paradox. My friends act like none of this is happening / attached to N3WCLOCK like an emotional-support pet. And yet, on the

track, stopwatches don't work / sprinters are measured only by
who finishes first.

No throwing today / we walk to the weight room together. It's
just Coach Aimee and the throwers here now. Kevin is flexing his
biceps and kissing them. Bill and Jon are fake-punching Kevin in
the back of the head. The three girls who've been throwing since
middle school walk together up front with Coach Aimee. They hate
me. As well they should.

PLYOMETRIC PUSHUPS

About an hour later, we're in the weight room and I've rotated
through all four machines, and I'm throwing a medicine ball to
Kevin and he's throwing it back. My core muscles feel stronger
than ever. My legs are ready / I may have found my biceps. Coach
Aimee yells, "Plyometrics!" and everyone but me drops to the
floor like they were shot.

I slowly lower myself down for a regular pushup. I do one. I
do another.

Then I do five plyometrics. Lower myself down, then push up
with all I got. Explode—that's the trick. Each time Coach yells,
"Explode!" I feel something familiar. I have exploded. I am probably still exploding. Forever.

FOREVER

Forever is a family thing. Blood thicker than water / forever. Always
look out for your own / forever. In our family, it's different. Mama
will be gone forever / sister will control us forever / AFT3RMATH.
We don't know what to do quite yet. In time, we'll figure it out /
take more dares / stop living in boxes.

WALKING ON SUNSHINE

Coach Aimee is part enthusiasm and part sociopath. Today, after we were done training, she made us run a lap backward around the track and she ran it with us while singing a song from the 1980s called "Walking on Sunshine." The three girls who hate me joined in. Must be a track thing. I don't plan on learning the words.

I'm in the locker room, stretching out my hamstrings one last time when my phone chimes with a text from inside my locker.

"Whose phone is that?" Coach Aimee asks.

I'm mid-stretch / pretend I don't hear her / she has a thing about phones.

When I walk past her office and toward the door, she says, "Nice work on the weights today. You're doing great." Giselle Masterson is sitting in the chair next to Coach Aimee's desk. She's the only one of the three thrower girls whose name I know.

Giselle says, "Amazing for someone who never did this before."

MY PHONE IS A DISEASE

Carrie stops her red Mini Cooper at the curb outside the locker room and I hop in, backpack on my lap.

"Salutations," I say. We take off past the tennis courts.

"I bombed that fucking essay question. My dad is going to kill me."

"He probably won't," I say. My phone chimes again to remind me.

"Who puts an essay question on a chem quiz?"

"It'll be fine. It's only a quiz."

"He's probably going to make me quit track."

"He won't," I say. "You're the best jumper we have."

Jumpers and throwers: the only way to measure track success
while stuck in a fold in time and space.

She turns up the music. I pull out my phone to check the text
that came in.

The text is from Richard / box #11.

It says: *something is wrong.*

WHAT YOU DON'T KNOW ABOUT BOX #9

My sister isn't allowed out of her hole.
My sister isn't allowed into her hole.
My sister is the hole.
My sister—the eddy / the hurricane
Us—the eye / hiding in the bathtub
My sister—a dog bite, ragged and hot
lies / teeth you always knew were there.
My sister in box number nine
is not in box number nine.
She hasn't lived here in six months.

But Daddy keeps a box for her
just in case.
It is locked from the outside.

WHAT YOU DON'T KNOW ABOUT BOX #9

Before my sister left,
she buried,
in the conduit / along the way,

a minefield. Because her escape
could not be clean.

Her hands achieved notoriety
as explosions.
Her memory had a reputation
for being spotty / switching teams /
being on the side that's winning.

My sister is never coming back.
Relief this big doesn't come often.

Floor Plan / Wiring Diagram

THE MAIN BOX

Daddy says to understand anything is to understand energy. He's an electrician, so this makes sense to him. When he looks at a house, the walls disappear and he sees only the paths of the wires / flow of energy.

Our house was built by precision machines—the conformity is alarming. Ring circuits of wall outlets in each room, each circuit to its own breaker in the basement. The labels in the main box are meticulous. LIVING ROOM, DINING ROOM, KITCHEN, BEDROOM 1, BEDROOM 2, BEDROOM 3, BEDROOM 4, BATHROOMS 1 & 2—all on one story. BASEMENT has its own breaker even though nothing is down there but old junk. Old junk and the main box containing the circuit breakers.

On the left side of the box are breakers for the major appliances. Usual suspects. WATER HEATER, FURNACE, AC, DRYER, WASHER, RADON UNIT, DISHWASHER and OUTDOOR SOCKETS. Below the breakers for the outlets and appliances live three lighting breakers. Every wire coming into the main box is straight / lines up with the others / like boarding-school attendance.

It's as if the development hired robot electricians.

To understand anything is to understand energy.

Daddy took me down to the main box the day after we moved in. He showed me all the breakers and when I called it a fuse box, he said, "Say consumer unit now. No more fuses."

"Can I call it the main box? Because consumer unit sounds too . . . uh . . ."

"Main box is fine," he said.

"What's that?" I asked, pointing to a diagram Daddy had tacked to the wall.

"It is drawing of electricity in house," he answered.

I squinted. This was what he saw when he looked at the house / the world / everything. There were a lot of shapes, but mostly forward slashes / like this / all over the place. "What are those?" I asked.

"Direction of energy. Switches turned on. My father told me these things." He taps his head. "Very smart man. Always moving forward."

—◻️—

To understand anything is to understand energy. If you don't know what your main box looks like, you don't know anything. No one ever looks at their main box. No one sees the connections, the pathways in the walls. No one cares. No one wants to know anything about energy. It's infuriating. It's the gunpowder. Not caring is the gunpowder.

—◻️—

After I climb through the me-shaped hole to box #7, I change from my sweaty track clothes and follow the plywood passageway to where it smells like food. Daddy is standing at the counter in the kitchen, chopping parsley. "You are never here for dinner, Truda."

I'm always here for dinner.

He says, "It is not boys, is it? Because I do not want you to throw away everything for some boy."

"I'm here for dinner. I'm literally setting the dinner table."

"Aha! It *is* boys!" he says.

"I was at track practice."

"Every night?"

I nod. "Every night."

"No boys?"

"No boys."

"Men eat women, Truda. It is fact of the world."

"I know," I say. "Don't worry."

"You are too important to be an American high school hors d'oeuvre. Stale crab. Fancy toothpicks." He waves his hand. "All this *fun and dumb.*" He sprinkles the parsley onto our dinners, slides a claw hammer from the pocket of his Carhartt work pants, then reaches into his back pocket and retrieves a nail. Climbs up / knees on the counter / hammers it into the plywood. Always moving forward.

DINNER FOR TWO

To understand anything is to understand energy.

"Where's Richard?" I ask.

"Had a class or something. Took car."

Good. Richard is free of box #11 for the night. That's what matters / *something is wrong.*

I spoon lasagna into my face and chase it back with garlic bread and green salad.

"What's the hurry?" Dad asks. He pours himself a glass of wine. Offers one to me, to be polite, as he's done to all of us since we were born, and then gets me a glass of water. "Tell me about school."

"I'm really excited about the meet next week. Nervous, too."

He nods. We eat.

"I mean school. Books. Do you need any help?"

"I'm good," I say. "Behind on one thing. A paper. I'll figure it out."

I get another square of lasagna and refill my glass of water.

Daddy says, "When is this meetup?"

I translate / chew. "The *meet* is next Tuesday."

"Why are you nervous?"

"I've never done one before."

He nods and takes a sip of wine. "You are a brilliant girl."

"Okay," I say.

"Grades not as good as Richard's, but you have creative ways of expressing yourself. This is your success."

Not everyone can be a rifle.

He says, "So you will do first meetup on Tuesday. Then another, then another. You make each one better. You grow. You win."

His lasagna keeps improving. His homemade vinaigrette. He is a walking example of growth mindset. And I am stuck inside a series of his boxes, even though I fly a thousand yards a day.

SIX WHOLE MONTHS

To understand anything is to understand energy.

I help Daddy put a plate aside for Richard and we do the dishes. I wash. He dries. The pristine dishwasher sits inches from us under the countertop wondering why my father sees it as some sort of threat to our family.

Dish-doing is his old-world way to show affection / model teamwork. It's the way he hugs. Continental-style table manners are how he shows love.

We finish cleaning up and I turn off the overhead light. He says, "How good are you—in this track?"

"I'm very good." I've never said this about anything, ever / would have caused a flash flood / twelve-alarm fire.

"Next Tuesday is my birthday, you know."

"I know," I say. "You don't have to come if you don't want to." I smile. He smiles.

He stands for a minute, smiling at me. My eyes wander around the partially boxed kitchen and out into the hallway / to the boxes around the switch / to the switch.

He says, "I will be there to show my pride for you."

I say, "Good night," and kiss him on his forehead.

To understand anything is to understand / energy is Paleolithic like I am / trying to survive. It's natural and enormous. It's earthquake and ocean. It's rumors and sunlight. Sometimes, it flows in all directions. Sometimes, it only flows in one. Here, in his series of plywood boxes, Daddy is still trying to contain our energy / keep us safe from doing things too well. But sister is gone now. Six whole months.

I look out my bedroom window and see the car in the driveway.

Richard is home. *Something is wrong.*

SWITCH LOGIC

Locate the switches.

In our precision-built development ranch home, lights are the only obviously switched energy sources. The switch units are mounted right on the wall at shoulder-height—exactly forty-eight inches from the floor—in every room. So convenient.

On. Off.

Richard is home. *Something is wrong.*

PEOPLE SWITCH

To understand anything is to understand energy.

It's not always lights, you know. You can switch an outlet. You can switch an appliance. You can switch anything, really. Even people.

Richard is home. *Something is wrong.*

OOO!

Sometimes when I was younger, I used to stick chewed gum into the eyes of wall outlets. You know the ones—two surprised little men stacked on top of each other—without whom our freezer melts, our hairdryer goes silent. Without them, your aquarium fish will die. Without those two little men—both saying "Ooo!" at the exact same time—there would be no TV / cold beer / online banking.

When you breathe, you don't need to be plugged into any-thing. The little men are in the walls, admiring your diaphragm. This is why I plugged their eyes with gum. The gum was handy / they were staring. One time, I covered their little mouths, too. No more "Ooo!" No more eyes. Just gum-covered outlets and energy with nowhere to go.

Richard is home. *Something is wrong.*

CONDUIT

The wire that connects the appliances and the outlets and the switches must, if not hidden inside the house's skin, be protected by conduit—a box for wire. A safe place. Like Daddy's boxes but tubular / long and thin and made of either metal or rigid plastic.

Because of Daddy's boxes, conduit now connects everything in our house. It is not safe for visitors. There are booby traps in our conduit / the house is laced with tiny, erratic bombs. Boom! On my way to the bathroom. Boom! Midnight carb snack. Boom! I lose my toes ten times a day. Boom! On my way to find Richard.

Box #11

SOMETHING IS WRONG

Richard is standing in his room with his arms crossed. He looks normal. He's not smiling, and he's not frowning, but that's our rifle / Richard. Emotions are not on the syllabus.

"She called me," he says.

This could be Mama or sister / probably sister if *something is wrong.*

"When?"

"When I got outside Maya's."

Maya still lives next door to our old townhouse—the one with a fuse box. Richard goes there to talk to Maya's mother, Karen, who is a social worker and therapist. She doesn't charge him / he doesn't tell her the whole truth. That's how the deal works.

"Why did she call you? What did she say?"

"She asked some weird shit about me and what classes I'm taking. She asked me about you. And if you and Carrie are still friends. She talks to Carrie," he says, "I think."

"I'm sure she said that, but it's probably not true," I say. "What else? Why did you text that something's wrong?"

He fiddles with the cuticle on his thumb for a second. "Mama's in rehab," he finally says. "She wanted to let us to know."

Mama is probably not in rehab.

We sit on his bed for a minute, side by side. He picks up a pair of dirty socks and tosses them toward his laundry basket.

"And she's working at a nursing home now," he says. Shivers. It causes me to shiver. Her energy understands how to move through us. "She's a cook."

Last time we talked about her, Richard reported that she was volunteering at a hospital, reading books to kids on the pediatric cancer ward.

"So she dropped out of college, I guess," I say.

He shrugs.

Richard has always been a smart rifle. He's not easily swayed by most people. Sister, though—alone in any space—serves as an individual corrective lens to each one of our family / diabolical / parts of us are hypnotized / who and which parts change on any given day.

"How are you, Richard?"

"I need to sleep," he says.

"I'm sorry she called you."

"I wish she'd just go away like she said she would," he says. I don't point out that he could just let the calls go to voicemail / he looks tired.

He gets into his single bed / clothes still on / shoes kicked off the edge. Snuggles with his duvet. Puts a pillow over his ear to block out the hammering. I marvel the light switch inside his bedroom door. I switch it to OFF and navigate the passageways from his room / #11 to my room / #7.

FOLKLORE

The last time my sister called me, five pretend-months ago, a month after she left for college seven hours away, she told me she'd called child services because Daddy was abusive. She said she would save me / I'd come to live on campus with her / she would take me to beer-keg parties.

Daddy never hurt any of us, not once. He's not even unkind. Sister has said he's an alcoholic, but there is no alcohol in our house aside from dinner wine. She said he's a drug addict. No drugs in our house aside from Advil and Mylanta. Sometimes she would hide the Advil when Daddy got low-air-pressure headaches.

Her weather is unpredictable.

Explosions aren't supposed to announce themselves.

When she was seven, she killed an injured bird with a screwdriver. Richard thinks about it a lot because he was there and tried to stop her. Something happened that day / changed Richard forever. His energy took form / rifles don't talk much.

I wish I knew Portuguese so I could have whispered something funny to Richard while he fell to sleep, instead all I said was "Sleep tight." That's what Mama would say when she'd close my door at night.

I wonder where she is if she isn't in rehab.

When I get back to box #7, which takes a while because Daddy's passageways are getting smaller / thicker / safer, I flop on my bed and open my laptop to write the thesis statement for my Solution Time paper. Nothing comes to me.

By the end of the month, I will figure out how to make people give a shit about other people. I still have no idea how I'll do this because I live in a house where emergencies are cubed like snack cheese and giving an actual shit has been put on hold. The hold music is shock. No time exists in shock / nothing can be done for us / no thesis statement for that / AFT3RMATH.

I close the laptop and stretch. It's soon time for work.

I wait until everyone is sleeping.

I bring a small crowbar.

Night Shift

ZENO OF ELEA

At rest / I am moving / with my crowbar.

ROBERT PLUTCHIK

Anger / Anticipation / the switch.

DIGGING

The switch is impossible to reach. There is new construction every day. To get to the switch I would have to disassemble the entire series of boxes—from #1 to #11—that now hold the first switch-protecting box in place. But tonight I want to see the supply, which I can see if I get through the drywall under the switch, which is easy to access by removing only one plywood side of the outer switch box.

BOOM! I get the panel off, but hit a tiny bomb. My hands are here, but my brain is exploding to the fact that Richard cannot be trusted. Exploding to the day I found him crying that first time, three years ago, I was still in middle school, he was a senior in high school and we agreed—never let her alone with us. Ever. But Richard cannot be trusted / he left me alone with her all the time. Had friends to do stuff with. Had senior year to complete / rifle to assemble.

He tried. He took me fishing. He'd rent a canoe on the lake and we'd take Daddy's rods and we probably used the wrong lures. We weren't really fishing.

Richard cannot be trusted. He is limp from a lifetime of game. The game is his life. There are no do-overs. Even though sister lit

him on fire and it's not his fault, he doesn't know what kind of lure
to use in the lake / scratches his burns / is not able to heal.

UNWIRING DIAGRAM

I poke the crowbar into the wall below the switch and I pull out
the drywall in dusty, prune-sized pieces and let them fall. I aim
the flashlight and look for supply wires. At first glance, there are
no wires going to the switch. I look again and there are a million
wires going to the switch. A billion wires. More wires than can fit
this house.

They start to flash / casino of possibility / impossibility. I can't
flip the switch tonight, anyway. Not while Richard is sleeping /
not while I'm training.

x equals not knowing what flipping the switch will do.

I replace the drywall, layer it with tape and glue, put the plywood piece back in place. Daddy will know someone was here /
he won't ask / will quietly grind dry peppers.

THE REAL WORK

I move to more private spaces and remove nail after nail.

Hall closet / garage / laundry room / the southeast hallway.
Some people do yoga to wind down. Some people smoke weed. I
disassemble the boxes / sometimes hanging trapeze-style upside
down / usually on my side. I only get four hours of sleep per night
/ hours don't exist / I am always awake / always asleep.

I am in Zeno's arrow. I feel *everything* / I feel *nothing*.

When I get back to box #7, I'm exhausted.

FLOOR PLAN / GPS

You don't understand the boxes and you don't want to. Plywood-ugly / nails too long. It's not a bedroom like you'd imagine—no curtains, no rug, no faux sheepskins—just wood grain / do not drag the soles. I've had a splinter in my foot so long that a callus has formed and the sliver will be encased forever / a fossil.

You don't understand the hallways and you don't want to. The construction feels dangerous. Energy moves through. We move through. We are the energy.

A million wires.

A picture for you / GPS. There are eleven boxes. Switch at the center, kitchen #3 north, living room #2, east of that. My box #7 southeast, Richard #11 southwest. Daddy sleeps northwest in the hallway. Everything is easier with directions. But nothing really comes with directions. Especially not our family.

There are clocks in each room so we know when to go to dinner / none of them move now / we are always on time. There is an alarm system in case of emergency. We have located our exits. Mine is through the me-shaped hole. Richard's is anywhere he can climb down the conduit / usually windows. Mama's was through the front door, two bags packed, yapping little dog under her arm, and three words. *Don't call me.*

That was nine months ago. Three days before time stopped. Everything has been different since / nothing seems real / no directions.

Daddy is not a precision machine / nothing is level. Full-time job making sure the energy runs right / quit his other job making mall kiosks / expert box-maker / two days after Mama left. In order: Mama left / he quit his job / time stopped. The order is important, I think. He never called Mama / obeys orders / to understand anything is to understand energy.

MAMA

Her weaknesses—American candy bars / American beer / American cheese / American shopping / American television—made her unintentionally lowbrow. She didn't mean for it to happen that way. She married a man from Somewhere Else who could not accept the *fun and dumb*.

Five years ago, she became an amateur psychic. Now, she's pay-per-minute, in-person, small groups at local hotel conference rooms. None of us expected this, considering she was always surprised when the mailman came. Not to say she's a fake. She may not be / to understand anything is to understand energy / it doesn't matter because she's not here.

We don't talk about the real reason she left / this explanation will do.

No one knows the real reason she left / this explanation will do.

Richard and I fought over her dinner chair.

She always sat to the left of Daddy, which put her out of sister's reach. Daddy settled the fight by putting me in Mama's old chair, and Richard took my old place, so sister's only way to touch us during meals was with her words.

It's very hard to eat while constantly exploding.

I think that's the real reason why Mama left. She used to drink

Mylanta straight from the bottle and by the time she said *Don't call me,* she'd been going to bed before eight o'clock for weeks. I knew she wasn't sleeping.

We'd been studying cancer in health class. Deep down, I suspected my mother had stomach cancer. So many bombs / too many years / Mylanta.

She's fine. No cancer. She wrote me an email a few days later when time stopped. Small talk, mostly, but then *I wanted to make it easier on your father. He works so hard, and when he would come home all he got was chaos. You had nothing to do with this.*

I replied to the email and told her I needed her.

I don't fit into the family. I heard all the reasons.

I replied and told her she was my mother, which meant she fit into the family / my family / I missed her.

Your father is devastated, but it's for the best.

I asked Richard, "If he's devastated and she's devastated, then why did she leave?"

Richard told me to wait / I wasn't sure for what.

She now lives in a small apartment she'd rented for her office / psychic den. It's got angels painted on the walls of the waiting room / smells like burnt sage. She sleeps on the futon couch surrounded by her crystals, where the next day, people will sit with cash hoping to contact their departed loved ones.

Daddy now relies on his old friend Carmichael for parenting decisions. Carmichael video-calls every pretend-Sunday, but Daddy refuses to use the camera / all Carmichael sees when he talks to Daddy is Daddy's ear. Carmichael talks loud, so I stay nearby when he calls. Whenever Carmichael mentions reaching out to Mama, Daddy hangs up.

All I know is Mama has the wrong idea about what's going on here / I don't know what's going on here / we're all in a daze. So I invented work for myself. Seems reasonable work. It will lead to something solid in the end / on / off.

By the time I climb into bed, I've collected 234 six-inch, galvanized, hot-dipped steel nails.

I still don't have a thesis statement.

Tomorrow is Trust.

BEST TEAM EVER

"Y'all know I have trust issues," Carrie says. "So every time we get to Trust, I go kinda numb. It's not really a good feeling for me."

Eric says, "Trust has a lot to do with what home is like and home sucks for you right now." Two Trusts ago, Eric would have never said something so empathetic.

"Carrie, what do you trust?" Ellie asks. "You trust me, right?"

Carrie sighs. "I trust all of you, but what I guess I'm saying is that when I think about trust, the way we do here, capital T, it makes me think about how few people I do trust. So then I get sad."

"I'm not going to force you to trust anyone," I say. I trust no one, not even Carrie, really, and she's my oldest real friend / fifth grade. "So how about things? You trust your car, right?"

"It's a dependable car," she says.

"What else?"

"I trusted this chair when I sat on it. And I trusted that school would be open today. I didn't trust that no one would steal shit from my locker," she says.

"That's only because you had that happen before," I say.

"Someone broke into your locker?" Len says. "That sucks."

"Eighth grade. Gym locker. Stole my favorite pair of jeans," Carrie says. "Never saw them again."

"So trust often depends on past experience, as established," I say.

"Sorry about your jeans," Ellie says. "You can never replicate a favorite pair of jeans."

"Agreed," Len says.

Carrie stops to explain the ideas in her class project about Zimbardo's time perspectives and how they affect us, especially relat-
ing to Trust. Well, her, specifically. She will fear her locker being
robbed because it has been robbed before because in regard to
locker-theft experiences, she has a "past-negative time perspective." Eric jumps in and explains that theoretically, she could still
have that lack of Trust even if her locker hadn't been robbed before because trauma that passes down via epigenetics can cause
children of people who had their locker robbed to have the dis-
trust naturally. Ellie adds that Trust is a tricky concept when viewed
through a child development lens because there are different levels
of trust. As a baby, you learn Trust when you are taken care of, but
by age ten, you have moral ideas and know, for example, that lying
is a barrier to Trust, even if someone is lying to you because they
think it's part of taking care of you.

"I wish Nigel was here to hear you guys talk," Len says, with
his camera out, recording. "You sound so fucking smart."

"Best team ever," Carrie says.

We high-five.

Nigel is suddenly talking at us through the intercom. "Psych
Team, check in."

We sound off, like saying "here" in first-grade attendance except we say Hello, Nigel in the most done-with-Nigel voices we can
manage.

"Are you geniuses coming up with anything? Your thesis statements are due next week."

We're in different climate zones. Nigel is a plant that grows in
places where things don't freeze and thesis statements matter /

delicate. We are five teenagers who grow in wild northern fucking Alaska trying to figure out what feelings are. We tell him we're
fine. He says we don't seem fine / that he's coming to class tomorrow to assess us.

He says, "Don't forget, your papers have to be twice as good as
everyone else's because you chose psychology," and the intercom
squeaks off.

They all look back to me as if Nigel never interrupted. I say,
"We're in Zeno's arrow. So I want you to really feel something.
Close your eyes. Think of a person you really admire, or the feeling of being admired. Or the feeling of being accepted or being
trusted. What do you feel about trustworthy things? I'll write
down anything you blurt out starting . . . now."

During the next half hour, the whiteboard fills with words and
phrases.

Proud, good, like I did something right, the feeling of giving yourself to someone
you trust, watching someone be awesome, sending thank-you cards when you mean it
(not when forced—Eric thinks this is evil), wishing you could be more like someone
and knowing you can, doing good deeds feels nice, helping someone by listening, not
gossiping, being accepted feels so good, being admired can feel fake (is that trust or
lack of it? or humility?—Len) makes me cry, makes me smile, makes me want to
do more good things, makes a person feel successful, when you trust someone it's like
being safe in your bed, having no fears, inspires hope, inspires more trust.

x equals how I don't know what Trust is.

The hardest thing about talking about Trust, we learn for the
third time, is that all of our minds go to lack of Trust because we
feel we have experienced that more than Trust. Carrie points out

again that this means we are past-negative according to Zimbardo. We debate—have we *really* been screwed over that many times or is it only a perception? *Where does being screwed over fit on this clock? Len: anger, fear, sadness, disgust. Eric: Surprise, too. Ellie: Nigel is a perfect example.*

We examine what makes someone trustworthy. *Mutual respect, good listener, good communicator, honesty, no gossip, knows when to let you cry (Ellie) and knows when to help you, and is happy to see you and see you succeed. In your corner, has your back, sticks up for you.*

x equals how I know what Trust is, but don't have any.

UNBELIEVABLE / PALEOLITHIC

I was warming up / long throws for fun. I felt energy everywhere and inside me and I saw the other throwers out on the field collecting their javs and goofing around. I didn't think my jav would go that far.

No one got hurt.

That's all that matters.

Coach Aimee says, "That's a fifty-meter javelin. It shouldn't even land point down at that distance." She hands me another jav and says nothing about how far it went.

This time everyone is watching. I run. I hop-step. I throw. I aim for the goal posts. It falls short and lands right in front of Giselle Masterson, flat landing / skid.

"That had to be a hundred fifty," Coach Turner says, jogging toward us. Coach Aimee barely looks up from her training schedule clipboard.

"I'm scared about next Tuesday," I blurt / energy gone wild.

"You'll do fine," Coach Turner says.

"I still don't know what a field judge is," I say.

Coach Aimee says, "We'll walk you through it. I promise."

"What if I throw at the wrong time?"

"I'll be there with you," Coach Aimee says. "I'll tell you exactly what to do."

"I still don't know when to get on deck or in the hole or whatever," I say.

"On hold," Coach Aimee corrects / looks so sick of me.

"Throw it again, kid," Coach Turner says.

I pick up the last of the javs and weigh it in my hand. I bounce on my feet. Energy is everywhere. It's like I'm pulling from a source underground. All that lightning that gets rerouted to the earth—green wires attached to metal poles—it's rerouting upward now. Into my feet. My legs. My back. My arm. Into the jav. I am the jav. I have to hold back, the way I've always held back. I fly right over the field with no wobble. Giselle Masterson shades her eyes with her hand / sees me closing in.

She runs / watches it land where she was standing. She looks over at us—Coach Turner, Coach Aimee, and me—and she picks up her gear by the shed and huffs out of the stadium and toward the locker room.

"Unbelievable!" Coach Turner says. "You really got something!"

"I'm Paleolithic."

I walk to the other end of the field and pick up my javs.

Giselle's two thrower friends greet me with something I'm not used to.

"Holy shit can you throw! Nice job!"

"Yeah—you're going to score us some serious points."

I look at them, unsure what to say.

"I get to concentrate on discus now. Can't thank you enough," the first one says.

"Me too," the other one says. "I can't even get close to beating you."

I am a lost / loose wire. I am a million wires.

"Why are you being so nice to me?" I ask.

TRACK TEAM

"You're good," one of them says.

"You've never been on-team before. We didn't know you."

"Oh."

"Giselle hates everyone," one says.

"Does that mean you do, too?"

"Her dad," one says, "was in the Olympics."

"That's cool," I say.

"He threw javelin," one says.

I don't know why her dad being an Olympic javelin thrower means Giselle should hate everyone / maybe that's why my Paleolithic survival spear almost hit her / to understand anything is to understand energy.

"Did he win medals?" I ask.

The two of them shrug and start collecting gear and putting it in the wagon. I walk to the shed to put the javs back. They follow, eventually. I don't know what to say to them. I see Carrie taking off her spikes on the bleachers, so I walk over and sit next to her.

"Dude. What the hell?" she says.

"Yeah. It's weird."

"How do you even do that?" she asks.

"I think it's energy. And time. I don't know. Something like that."

BIG MAC MEAL

"I'll have a Big Mac meal with a vanilla shake, please," Carrie says into the speaker.

She gives me one more chance to order / I decline.

Once we get the food, she drives to her house a few minutes away and we go inside. Carrie's house is normal. It's in a development, like ours is, but there is no exposed plywood and no mystery switch on the wall. Carrie has never seen the inside of my house. From the outside, I'm sure it looks fine.

She starts eating and I call Daddy.

"I came home with Carrie because her parents aren't home," I say.

Daddy says, "We have sausage for dinner. I will save for you."

"Thanks."

"Are you studying?" he asks.

"We just got here. But yes. I'm working on my paper."

He tells me to be home in an hour and I hang up.

Carrie says, "You still can't figure out a thesis statement?"

"I'm stalling."

"It's just a paper," she says. "It's not like we're really going to figure out how to save the world, you know. It's just a distraction from this time thing."

Time thing. Eight billion of us / no wristwatches / no way to break the record in hurdles no matter if you're in Bali or Botswana. Always 0623202016:44 / we are molecules floating in time / we are resting arrows / *time thing.*

"I don't know," I say. "Maybe."

I walk around her kitchen. It's nothing like our kitchen. Our kitchen is eat-in and small. Hers has nowhere to eat as a family, but a huge island and breakfast bar in the middle. Everything is marble.

"So, why is Giselle Masterson such a bitch?" I ask.

She chews and swallows. Washes it down with milkshake. "Um. She's probably only a bitch to you," she says.

"What's that mean?"

She looks at me with her head tilted like I should know what she's talking about. "You don't know?" Always the last one to know / this is not new / AFT3RMATH.

I hold my hands out and shrug.

Carrie takes a deep breath. "I don't even know how to tell you this if you don't know," she says, "but . . . there's a pretty popular rumor that your brother used to . . . um . . . be with Giselle. When he was a senior."

I do math. Richard is twenty-one and Giselle is a sophomore in high school. "No," I say. "There's no way anyone would even believe that."

She ugh-sighs. "The story goes that he picked her up at the rec center in the morning after her dad dropped her off."

"That's, like, six in the morning."

"Yeah. He took her to some parking lot and they . . . you know," Carrie says.

"What? Talked about pre-algebra?"

"You know."

"That's the stupidest thing I ever heard."

She nods and shoves a fist of fries into her mouth.

"Your sister told the whole school he was always like that," she says.

A thousand tiny bombs / "She's a liar," I say.

"Well, yeah. She eventually told me it was a lie and she was just mad at him for making her walk to school."

"But people still believe it?"

"Big rumor, little town," she says.

I sit and stare into space / time stops all over again / "Huh."

"Sorry to have to tell you that."

"No wonder Giselle hates me," I say. I send good-energy to Giselle Masterson, wherever she is.

Carrie adds, "She probably doesn't even remember. It's not like anything actually happened. But maybe you could tone it down a bit. I've been in track since seventh grade with Giselle. She was always the star. This is probably freaking her out."

When Carrie drives me to my house I can feel a new energy between us. Like she's mad at me for an old rumor / for throwing so far / tone it down a bit.

REST

Daddy has installed an intercom system from wherever-he-is to the kitchen.

"Plate is in oven," he says through a speaker.

"Thank you." I put a mitt on and get it from the oven.

"You smell like fast food."

I decide not to hear him / believe he can smell me through a speaker. I walk to the wall unit / turn the volume all the way down. I'm thinking about Richard and Giselle Masterson / rumors / sister. I'm thinking about how everyone knows more than I do about everything. I'm thinking about my thesis statement. I don't know why they make us work so hard on something so impossible. I'm tired. We're all tired.

I think about Zeno and arrows. Motion / Time. All of us stuck in a single resting moment, not resting. I don't think I've ever rested in the sixteen years I've been alive. I'm not sure any kid does.

Maybe if we knew what it was like to rest, we would understand time better.

Fear

WHAT YOU DON'T KNOW ABOUT NIGEL

I'm not ready for Solution Time today. Was up too late failing at finding a thesis statement / succeeding at pulling 189 more nails.

It's pretend–St. Patrick's Day and the school is more green than usual. Eric is wearing a kelly-green polo shirt. Len is wearing forest-green boots. Nigel is here / smells like green gin. He's standing with his arms crossed with a smile on his face like burnt toast.

"This whole team is a waste of time," Nigel says.

"Ironic," Eric says. We giggle.

On / off / Nigel explodes.

He levels eyes with Eric. "If this is so funny, then tell me how this time paradox is going to work out for your dad. If a two-year sentence is stuck in time, how long will it be before you see him again? Didn't think of that, did you?"

None of us knew that Eric's dad was in prison / not dancing to Cuban music while he makes dinner with Eric's mom. Shit. Nigel is an asshole. I want to erase his mouth.

WHAT YOU DON'T KNOW ABOUT NIGEL'S MOUTH

My mother kept my
childhood drawings of
fish and horses and one time,
a bird.
She wrote the dates
on the back and put them
in a box.

There are ten family pictures.
I drew one each year
on my birthday
because I like tradition.
In all ten,
sister has no mouth.

"You guys don't know *anything* about the world! You haven't had to pay bills or suffer at all. You haven't experienced being *successful.* I've worked for twenty years and my peers call me a *transformational teacher.* What do they call you? You're just a bunch of cocky kids who think you know shit when you haven't even been out of the county," he says.

Nigel is showing his whole ass here. All of us have left the county. Most of us have been out of the country. Three of us have dual passports. Eric's mom is from Argentina. Len's mom is from Lagos.

"You know," Nigel says, "when I go to Nepal, I see things none of you would . . ."

Len texts me. *You know he just broke up with Ms. Moreland, right? Dude's going nuts from too much semen.*

I text back. *What a douche. I can't believe he just said that to Eric.*

Dude is high on himself.

Really? Moreland?

Yup.

Why do I never know this kind of gossip?

I'm a documentarian. It's my job to know things.

Carrie elbows me. Nigel has stopped talking about his travel adventures. He has asked a question.

Ellie says, "Today Tru was going to talk to us about Fear for the last time. Her project is really interesting, Nigel. All of ours are."

I never thought Ellie would be the one to stick up for us, but Eric is still staring at his jeans.

"Do you know what other teams are doing right now?" Nigel says. "STEM—you know—actual science?"

"Psychology is science," Len says.

Nigel looks up toward the ceiling / cycling through energy / on / off / on.

"You know what, Leonard?" Nigel kicks the nearest chair and sends it sliding across the floor / crashing into the other chairs and desks like bumper cars. BOOM! "I'm sick of your shit. I'm failing you. I'm failing you all." He looks at his phone for a moment and then walks out the door / slams it louder than I've ever heard a door slam.

By the time Ellie stops pacing / Carrie's eyes stop leaking, Len has already uploaded the video of Nigel's tirade from his phone and trimmed it to a perfect fifteen-second clip. Eric has texted his mother and told her that Nigel just told the entire class that his dad is in prison. I have picked up the kicked chair from the floor and it's full of frantic energy.

Today is Fear.

Nigel is Fear.

We just did Fear / today.

PIAGET'S FIFTH STAGE / STUDY HALL

If you're not careful with your energy—your attention—you run the risk of becoming judgmental. I wonder if Jean Piaget ever came up with a developmental stage for that. When, exactly, do humans become superior assholes? Or is that just called adulthood?

I look up the worksheet that Ellie gave us in pretend-November about Jean Piaget and his theory. The basic four stages are Sensorimotor (birth–2 years old), Preoperational (2–7), Concrete Operational (7–11), and Formal Operational (12 and up).

There are scientists who disagree with Piaget's theory of cognitive development, so I read their arguments against it. Some psychologist in 1979 said that an average of 40–60 percent of college students couldn't handle Piaget's stage-four formal operations at all. Another dude in 1994 claims that only one-third of adults ever reach the formal operational stage, which means two-thirds of adults are unable to grasp abstract concepts or use logic to test out ideas. That means there are twelve-year-olds that are more developed than Nigel, considering Nigel has yet to handle the abstract idea that when his peers told him he was a transformational teacher, they were probably pranking him / keeping him happy so he didn't kick chairs around.

Carrie drives me home after track practice. We didn't throw today, probably on account of Giselle Masterson acting like I tried to skewer her on purpose at practice yesterday. We trained / I leg-pressed my own weight / Kevin knocked me over with a medicine ball but I'm fine.

"I hope I didn't freak you out last night," she says. "I didn't want to freak you out."

"Nah. You didn't," I lie. "I don't know how anyone believes my sister about anything. Plus, Richard has literally never had a girlfriend. Like, ever."

"That's part of it. Don't you think that's creepy? To like—never have a girlfriend? At his age?"

I shrug in frustration.

"Big rumor, small town, that's all," she says.

She gives me a sympathetic look and drops me at the curb.

I walk to the me-shaped hole and climb up.

PIAGET'S DINNER MENU

It's a Sensorimotor kind of dinner tonight. Three infants sit down to roast pork with gravy, mashed potatoes, and a heap of cauliflower. We spoon-feed one another.

I give Daddy a spoonful of mashed potatoes. "I had a good day in school today."

He clears food from my chin with a rubber-coated spoon. "That is very nice."

Richard feeds Daddy a spoonful of pork. "I got an A on my literature exam."

Daddy lifts him up, pats him gently on the back, and burps him. "Very good, boy."

We never removed the other chairs. There are two infants here you can't see, but you can taste them in the food / residue.

"How was your practice today, Truda?" Daddy asks.

"Good. We trained inside, mostly. One girl won't talk to me, but everyone else is nice."

"Is she not able to talk?"

"She talks to her friends. Hates me," I say. "Richard probably knows more about that than I do."

Richard looks confused.

"Giselle? Masterson?" I say.

Richard tugs on his bib / his lip quivers. "I don't like this cauliflower."

Daddy says, "You never did, son."

"Why do you make it, then?"

"Because Truda and I both like cauliflower."

"Do I have to eat it?"

"You are a man now. You can choose not eat the food I have made for you."

Richard shrinks. Eats the cauliflower.

Before I go to bed, I pull 203 more nails.

NEW TIME

N3WCLOCK was still the leader in time simulation, but other clocks had been invented by the day Nigel came to scare us all about becoming anything like him.

In pretend-September, a university class in Japan invented OURCLOCK, which attempted to get people to live in backward-time. Their theory was that if we moved backward until we reached June 23, 2020, we would make up the time we lost. Or gained. Or something like that. It made world news, but no one used it.

In pretend-October, four women in a grad studies program at Trinity College Dublin invented U-CLOCK, a time simulator that reflected the natural rhythms of your body. "Some people are night owls. Some people love sunrises. We no longer have to live by a clock set by men. We can decide for ourselves," the leader of the group said. They made and sold an app that could, through artificial intelligence, make a personal clock for everyone. It worked well, made them a lot of money, and yet no one was able to agree on a time to meet for dinner or drinks. Schoolchildren arrived to their classes anytime they wanted and U-CLOCK was their excuse.

N3WATCH

At the end of pretend-November, right after pretend-Thanksgiving, the owners of N3WCLOCK sent legal documents to anyone who attempted to make an online time simulator claiming that all were a violation of trademarks and patents. At a TV news conference, the nineteen-year-old CEO wore a watch. He showed it to the camera.

N3WATCH became the best-selling holiday gift of all time. It beat the Rubik's Cube by a hundred million sales.

In pretend-February, N3WCLOCK finally sold their time to most major broadcasters and their logo and time showed in the top right corner of 75 percent of the stations on TV. Their price was a billion dollars / if you ever wondered how much time costs.

I'm not sure how students at other high schools were handling Solution Time, but by the time pretend–New Year came, all of us knew we'd never invent anything that would solve the actual problem.

We kept going because we knew we'd be graded. I kept going because I wanted people to give a shit about other people. Thousand-dollar N3WATCHes made it harder. Billion-dollar time made it harder. Nigel's bullshit made it harder.

HUMAN KILOWATT-HOURS

What I notice most is the increase in energy. In me. In the world around me. It's as if energy goes crazy sitting still. It doesn't know where to go / creeps up my arm / into the jav / into whiteboard markers. It creeps around everyone, all the time. Energy goes in. Energy comes out.

It's not the same kind of energy that runs a light bulb.

It's stronger.

Nigel wouldn't accept this as a fully formed idea because there's no proof. But time and energy have something in common. I just don't know what it is, yet. The AFT3RMATH is slowly coming to an end / I feel okay / first time in my life. Success was never possible before / this time / this energy / success is possible now.

WHAT ENERGY IS

On pretend-Thursday at lunch I say to Carrie, "The only energy measurement that humans seem to care about is calories."

"As opposed to?"

"Kilowatt-hours."

"What the fuck is a kilowatt-hour?"

"Exactly. But I bet you know how many calories are in that Snickers bar."

She looks at the nutrition facts. "Two hundred and fifteen."

"What does that mean?"

"It means that if I eat this, I will have to run the track three extra laps at four hundred miles per hour to burn it off," she says.

"Could you power a light bulb with it instead?"

"Before or after I eat it?"

"Before."

Carrie inspects the half bar in her hand. "What—like stick little probes in there? A positive and a negative? Use it like a battery?"

"You just made that up," I say.

She nods and says, "Let's stop talking about calories."

Carrie has been on antidepressants for six months. She's gained eighteen pounds. The people who point out this weight gain to her far outnumber the people who ask how she's feeling today, or if she feels like dying anymore.

"Sorry," I say. "I think you look great."

"My ass is huge."

"Huge asses are in fashion and I hate to tell you, but you are not otherwise fashionable."

She smacks me on my arm.

I smack her back.

"So how would you power a light bulb with Snickers?"

"Burn it," I say.

She eats it instead.

THUNDER AND OLIVES

As the rest of the school day goes by / chem / algebra II / health III, I track my energy. I write notes about it in class / ignore the lessons.

> x equals how my hands are glowing.
> x equals there is actual light coming out of my hands.

I feel somehow bigger than I am. I feel stronger. I maybe bumped my head when I fell over yesterday in the weight room / medicine ball could have shifted something. Nigel's anger-chair could have transferred wattage to me. Or Richard's intense dislike of cauliflower. I feel brighter than I ever have before.

Five minutes late to the track and Coach Aimee acts like I robbed a gas station. Makes me apologize. Tells me I should pay better attention to time / there is no time.

Yesterday, I would have just felt like an asshole for being late. Today, I say, "You know, you could have asked why I was late."

She makes me run four miles for my mouth.

> x equals how I'm sure the energy is building.
> x equals how other people can't see me glowing.

I don't feel a single step of the four miles. Time has stopped. In the arrow. My running is coming from the same place as thunder and olives / gifted by dirt.

I get to throw three times.

"You need more bounce on that last step," Coach Aimee says.

I use more bounce.

"You need more height in the throw," she says.

I give more height.

"You need to follow through," she says.

I follow through.

PLUTCHIK'S DINNER MENU

The starter will be Joy. You will eat it and feel instantly better. You belong here, you happy thing, you Mona Lisa smile, you fluffy kitten / newly hatched chick / baby bunny.

Daddy has music playing. He likes Ethiopian music. He likes Icelandic music. He likes everything but country and jazz.

"Tonight is curry!" Daddy says.

My phone chimes from my pocket. A text from Carrie. *Don't forget uniforms come tomorrow!*

"You don't like curry?" he says.

"I love your curry."

"Good," he says, and swings his hips to the beat. He is a very bad dancer. "What new thing did you learn today?"

x equals Joy, Trust, Fear, Surprise, Sadness, Disgust, Anger, and Anticipation.

x equals energy stuck in time.

"Psychology, mostly."

"Is it true we only use ten percent of this?" He taps his head / makes a goofy face.

"I have no idea."

"You seem—down."

"Just tired. Thursday. I'll probably go to bed early tonight," I say.

Daddy is making dough. He still calls it "duff" to be funny. When he first learned English, he made that mistake a lot before someone corrected him. "I felt so dumb," he told us back when I still played with dolls, "but English is difficult, and tough and rough are said same way, so who cares?"

He kneads / folds. Kneads / folds. Then he rolls the dough in his stiff palms to make balls. "Chapati!"

I say I have to go to my room and do some homework.

"You will miss best part! They puff on open flame!"

Daddy always said he liked American optimism until he moved here. "From over there, they look so proud and successful. But on closer view, they are discouraged and hiding failure." He sounds judgmental when I quote him, but English is not his first language and Daddy is very direct. Fact: I don't know many Americans that get as genuinely optimistic about making dinner as my dad.

I stay at the kitchen table, open my laptop, see the colorful Plutchik wheel, and I open a new document and start writing. Thesis statement: People would give a shit about other people more if they understood their own emotions. This has nothing to do with time. This thesis statement is bullshit. This paper is bullshit. This class is bullshit. Close my laptop. Watch the chapati puff up on the open flame. Daddy squeals every time it happens.

The main course is Trust. You will look around the dinner table and be ventral / vulnerable / calm. You belong here, in this trustworthy place.

Richard sets the table with a small book opened in his left hand. The book is *Lolita* by Vladimir Nabokov. I've never read the book, but I know what it's about / wonder why Richard is reading it / big rumor / small town. I fill water glasses as Daddy prepares plates. He has shredded carrot and cut orange slices and serves fresh yogurt.

Richard is already sitting, book still in his left hand. He ignores us and reads.

"Did you make this yogurt?" I ask.

"I did! It is a terrific thing!" Daddy says.

I hug Daddy.

Richard says, "The food is getting cold."

Daddy says, "The food will not get cold."

Richard looks up from his book and he is blank / not trustworthy / not here.

The side salad is Fear. You will feel paranoid that you trusted in the wrong place. You will wonder if Richard is someone else. You will hide it behind your Trust-smile and the kitchen will fill with the sounds of forks on old-world ceramic.

Richard says, "Sorry to read at the table. I have a big test."

Daddy and I nod.

Minutes pass. The yogurt is the most honest thing at this table.

The yogurt is the truth.

DISHWASHER

"Why don't we ever use the dishwasher?" Richard asks. His book is finally not in his left hand. He got carrot on it at dinner.

Daddy and I ignore him. My hands wrist-deep in hot soapy water / reality—I know the dishwasher doesn't really matter.

"Go study," I say. "We have it covered."

He stands for a moment watching Daddy and me wash and dry dishes. Neither of them seems to notice that I'm glowing / to understand anything is to understand energy.

"Go!" Daddy says to Richard. "Study!"

Richard walks to the new southwest plywood passageway and climbs in / toward box #11.

By the time we're standing at the doorway to the kitchen, lights off, countertop wiped down and dried, Daddy and I both exhale with satisfaction and he kisses me on the forehead, which makes me feel five and safe.

The doorbell rings.

This is shocking.

AT LEAST SHE DIDN'T BRING THE DOG

My mother—she's insatiable.

"Give your mother a hug," she says.

I comply.

"Tell me how you're doing in school."

I comply.

"Why are you so sweaty?"

I tell her I'm in track.

"Where's your brother?"

Daddy steps into the foyer and says, "Richard is studying for important exam."

"I need to see him."

Daddy and I just stand there. I have a thesis statement to write. Daddy has nails to hammer. Mama is not in rehab.

"Holy hell, what are you doing to the house?" she says, after noticing that Daddy's diorama of conduit and plywood has expanded tenfold since she last saw it.

"Go find Richard," Daddy says. He puts on his toolbelt and climbs into the east plywood passage. Opposite direction from Richard.

She looks at me. "How the hell am I supposed to find Richard?"

"Go that way."

She looks me up and down, inspecting, then looks at Daddy. "What is he doing to you?" she whispers.

"Stop," I say. "Just stop."

She definitely got a phone call from my sister this week, too.

"I miss you," I say.

"I worry about you," she says.

She looks me up and down again. I know my hair is dried-sweat stuck to my head and Mama isn't used to anyone being sporty. Even in all her American glory, she could never get into sports / can't see me glowing.

I hug her again. She smells like sandalwood incense and chicken nuggets. "It's so good to see you," I say.

"It's been a while," she says.

"It has."

"We should email more," she says.

"I'd rather you lived here."

"Your dad has it all worked out, right?"

I laugh. "He's barely managing," I say. I feel bad, but it's true. Carmichael gives him tips on how to save money with coupons and what temperature the freezer should be / not how to raise children / me.

"What about Richard?" she asks. "How is he?"

"Seems fine. Doing good in college."

"Does he have a girlfriend yet?"

"Not that I know of," I say.

"He really should. You know?" she says, mostly to herself.

She's not usually this flustered or uptight. One thing about Mama is that she could float through stress without flinching / until she couldn't anymore / Mylanta / this explanation will do.

"You could at least give me directions," she says, looking at the open ends of four different uneven pathways.

I point to the northwest hall. Not the right one. It would get her to Richard eventually, but only if he wants to be found.

As she inches through, I hear the tiny bombs explode inside the plywood / Daddy is saving us all even when he pretends not to notice / pretends not to be here. He forgets that we remember what it's like for him not to be here.

In the months before Earth entered the fold in time and space, Daddy was working at a cabinetmaker's shop / cash pay / good money. Until his boss took on a contract too big for them / the mall kiosk job / it changed our whole family. Daddy would go in at six in the morning and come home for dinner and then get in a van with his workmates and drive from Pennsylvania to Staten Island Mall to install the kiosks overnight while the mall was closed. He wouldn't get home until five in the morning. His boss, high on stress and coffee forgot time / forgot sleep / made the guys come in again at seven to make more kiosks / install / make / install. Daddy / no sleep for weeks / wife then gone from his bed / finally said no.

The problem wasn't in his quitting. The problem was in who occupied the most space in our house while he was off at the Staten Island Mall working for overtime pay / he was too tired to pick a side / implied there were sides / Mama left / then he quit / then time stopped.

They've got to work something out soon. Without each other, they're not okay / we're never going to get out of this / to understand anything is to understand energy.

300

It's late and I've got my crowbar and I'm nowhere near Mama and Daddy's old room, but I can hear them talking. Laughing about something. Enjoying each other's company / happiness and old times / friends catching up.

I pull 300 nails and Mama's car stays in the driveway until morning.

Mama

TROJANS
Daddy isn't in the kitchen for breakfast. There's no note. No sign of Richard.

I grab my packed lunch and a glass of homemade banana-mango-and-strawberry smoothie and gulp it down until my head aches from the cold / homemade-yogurt honesty.

I stuff all my books and gear into my backpack and slide through the me-shaped hole and go to the high school. I try to forget about Mama and how she didn't even seem happy to see me last night / this explanation will do.

x equals I don't know the truth about anything.
x equals I have come to depend on dairy products for trust.

It's a nice morning. Going to be warm. We get our uniforms today. I will officially be, after nearly three years in this high school, a *Trojan*. Yes, I know that's a brand name for condoms. Everyone knows that / some Trojan schools have even changed their mascot. What's sad is that most people don't even know what a Trojan really is. But they know there was a war. They don't know who won it or where it was, but who cares—let's make another condom joke.

PLUTCHIK'S LUNCH MENU
My father usually packs my lunch with love and Joy, but we have moved past that part of Plutchik's wheel of emotions. The leftover curry with basmati rice, yogurt, and shredded carrots is Surprise.

I am so happy to see it, it's as if Daddy packed a new puppy / old friend / trip to Aruba into this small rectangular container. Not the same sort of Surprise as seeing my mother last night / maybe this is why the yogurt tastes too tangy.

"What's your problem?" Giselle Masterson sits down in the empty chair at our lunch table and aims her words in a razor-whisper.

I look at her the way you'd expect.

"Nigel says you're telling people that you're going to kick my ass at the meet."

After I find my mandible, I say, "I've literally never said anything about you to anyone. Except Carrie," I say.

Carrie hears her name and stops talking about chemistry with Ellie and Eric.

"Well, he says you can't wait to crush me," Giselle says.

"I'm not a crusher," I say / still don't know what a field judge is.

Carrie says, "She is so not a crusher, Giselle."

Ellie says, "Nigel's the crusher."

We all sit for a moment, considering.

"He's such a dick to our group," Giselle says. "He says he's going to fail us all."

Ellie says, "He just loves drama."

Eric is on his phone. Carrie is nodding. I'm still swimming too far out, wondering why Giselle Masterson is talking to me.

"Did he yell and get all self-righteous?" Carrie asks.

"Did he talk about Nepal?" Ellie adds.

"Transformational teacher?" Eric says, without looking up from his screen.

"Yes! All of it!" Giselle says. "God, what an asshole. I thought he was only like this to us."

Eric, still looking at his phone, says, "We talk about it in science club. He's like that with everybody."

Giselle seems new to this information. Frankly, I am, too. We both say "Huh" at the same time.

Carrie looks around the room. Slaps her palms on her thighs and smiles. She stands up, steps on her chair, then onto the table, which wobbles a bit and Ellie holds it steady / Paleolithic logic.

Carrie claps the school clap. We've all known it since first grade. Two fast claps, pause, then three, pause, then four / Go Trojans. The cafeteria joins in until everyone is clapping and looking at our table. I see Len slowly walking toward us, camera up.

"Quick show of hands. Who else is being threatened that they're going to fail Nigel's bullshit?"

Hands shoot up. Everywhere. I try to see whose hand isn't up / everyone's hand is up. We are all failures because we have yet to get strip-searched in the Katmandu airport.

Carrie thanks them and sits back down.

Giselle says, "We're not going invent anything that actually solves it, right? It's like writing a fantasy story. That's what my paper looks like. A fucking fantasy thesis."

"Tru's also been stressed about the paper," Carrie says, trying to pull me to shore.

They look at me.

"I can't figure out a thesis statement. Plus, my idea is stupid," I say.

"Nigel made you think that," Carrie says.

"What's your idea?" Giselle asks.

I feel so embarrassed / wish I was able to stop time and sprint out of the cafeteria.

Carrie motions at me.

"I think we should all give more of a shit about each other," I say. "I think time stopped because none of us really give a shit about anyone else . . . or even ourselves."

Giselle stares at me for two solid seconds. "That's fucking epic," she says.

"Impossible to write about, though," I say. "Plus, who cares anyway? Life isn't any different. N3WCLOCK has most people not even thinking about why this is happening."

"Why do you think it's happening?" Giselle asks.

"The universe noticed we're falling apart and we need to learn how to rest."

As she considers this, I also consider it. I connect my ideas: We can't give a shit about ourselves or others unless we know how to rest / this is what the arrow is for. That's the most blunt I've ever been about it / the sitting-still energy moves through me and I feel warmer than usual / almost cry.

"Oh-kay," Giselle says.

Carrie says, "Why do you think it's happening?"

Giselle says, "My dad says it's just some weird glitch in the universe that humans shouldn't bother themselves with. He says we're too small to understand anything so big and that we're too big-headed to accept that it has nothing to do with us."

"I kind of agree," I say.

"Me too," Carrie says.

Ellie says, "Yeah."

Giselle adds, "I just need this fucking class to stop."

Len says, "I could do so much good with an extra two hours a day."

Everyone agrees.

Psych Team has fully assembled at the lunch table now that Len is here. We look at one another. Without a word, we plan the downfall of Solution Time / Nigel / the need for my thesis statement.

Giselle turns back to me before she leaves and says, "You won't crush me on Tuesday. Just so you know."

"I know," I say.

FIELD JUDGE

I have two school days until my first track meet. It took a whole hour to hand out uniforms and make sure everyone had the right size shorts.

I ask Coach Aimee about field judges at the end of practice.

"All they do is measure, mark the book, and tell you what to do. It's easy."

"But what if—like—if Coach Turner is right about me throwing so far—I mean—what if they disqualify me?" I ask.

"Why would they disqualify you?"

I shrug.

"Are you cheating?" she asks / too loudly.

"No."

"Then don't worry about it. You'll be fine."

I look at my hands.

As I climb up the me-shaped hole to box #7, I consider asking Daddy to cover it / locked from the inside / locked from the outside. Remove the escape. Remove the throw—the possibilities that come with being Paleolithic / trade in my favor before I flip my own switch and show people what I am.

x equals I don't know what I am.
x equals my mother's car still in the driveway.

UNIFORM

Our uniform tops are blue and purple, Trojan cool colors. Plutchik's colors for Sadness and Disgust. Which is how I feel in this uniform. Makes no sense / I'm fine / usually wear big sweatshirts.

"Truda?"

It's my mother. Her name is Concordia, but she calls herself Connie / says this to every client before they walk out of the angel room and into her crystal ball.

"Can we talk?" she asks through the door.

I put a hoodie on over my uniform and sit on my bed next to my backpack, pretending to get ready to do homework, but really I'm starving.

When she comes in, she tries not to look shocked. "It's like you live in a barn," she says.

"You get used to it."

She sits on my desk chair. "Tell me how you are."

I can't tell her about me / she can't see me glowing.

"Why won't you move home?" I ask. "Daddy really needs you. I need you. Richard needs you."

She seems uncomfortable with the truth / doesn't answer.

"I read our old emails a lot," I say. "You kept saying that you 'heard all the reasons.' And I think I know what you heard. I think they were lies."

"You're too young to—"

"You're stuck," I say. "You're stuck because you believed those lies."

She takes a deep breath and tears form in the corners of her eyes / mascara flakes floating on two little seas. "I know what was said about me," she says.

"That's the thing. You *don't* know. Nothing *was said* about you. We didn't even have a family meeting. Time stopped. We all got hooked on TV news and trying to figure out what was going on."

"I can't be where I'm not wanted," she says.

"Those were lies."

"Ask your brother. He still hates me."

"That's called triangulation," I say.

"You're sixteen. How do you know about triangulation?"

"Psych Team—in school. I know a lot about stuff like this. You'd be surprised."

She cups her chin in her palm. "Tell me more."

"Richard still talks to her. I think you still talk to her, too. If I'm right, then that makes a triangle," I say.

"She talks to Richard?"

"She called him on Monday. Told him you were a drug addict and in rehab," I say.

The look a mother gets when you are the messenger of lies / fury. "What the actual fuck?"

"And she called you on Monday, too. From what you said to me last night, I'm guessing she told you that Daddy is abusive—again." I roll my eyes.

"You're good," she says. Her eyes dart around the room as she puts puzzle pieces in their place. "She did call me on Monday. Told me you were in danger. That's why I'm here."

"I'm not in danger, and none of us ever wanted you gone."

"She did."

"She wants us all dead," I say / think of the bird / it was very alive when I saw it last—just an injured wing. "Because something's wrong with her."

"I tried everything," Mama says / there are ten screwdrivers stuck in her head / she removes them one by one. "Since she was a kid, you know? Therapy. More therapy. Group therapy. All secret because your father—well—you know."

My father doesn't believe in American psychology / thinks families should solve their own problems / hammers nail after nail after nail.

"I want you here and always have. And Daddy. He can barely function without you."

Mama blinks and the tears and flakes of mascara tumble down her cheeks.

"We need you," I say. "We love you."

"I'm just crazy," she says, "with my crystals and all my bullshit. Remember?"

"Yeah, no one ever said that about you."

"I'm the problem in the family because I—I—"

"You are totally not the problem in this family," I say. "Never were."

"I tried," she says. "I don't know what I did wrong."

"You didn't do anything wrong. You're a great mom," I say. "Don't you remember how we talked about this before? A week before you left. When Daddy was at that job all the time and she wouldn't stop gunning for you? I told you to just block her out. Pretend she isn't talking. Don't take anything personal. That's how Daddy taught me to deal with her, and it worked." I give her a moment to stop looking lost / stop being brainwashed. "We really need you to move back. We miss you."

She puts her face into her hands / takes a deep breath / wipes her cheeks.

"My next client is on Monday," she says. "I have to see my shaman before then. Get a soul retrieval or something. I need time to think." She pulls a tissue from her shirtsleeve and pats her cheeks dry / blows her nose. "I'll talk to your dad about coming back after that. I don't know if he wants me here. And look at this place! I don't want to live in a barn."

"We can fix it. But right now, I'm the only one in this house in the aftermath. I need you here with me."

"We're all in the aftermath," she says.

"Not if you're getting phone calls and not if you're believing the lies. Sorry. I'm not trying to be a jerk. But it's true. You can't be in the aftermath until you leave it behind."

She nods. "How did you get to be so smart?"

See how we skirt the town of our life—round and round on a plywood bypass / circle the problem like we can corral it / wild horses / dead birds / notes that read *Dear Truda, I hate you.*

"I'm starving," I say. "Can we go to the kitchen?"

When my mother gets up from the chair, she acts as if she's wearing a gown with a bustle, picks up the fabric and fluffs it out to her sides / Concordia / goddess of peace in a slipshod barn.

As we inch through the narrow plywood passage to the kitchen, Mama says, "All this building he's doing! It was an okay hobby, I guess. But now it's . . . not . . . um . . . very conventional, you know? The place looks crazy!"

"It's what he does to survive. He has to survive the lies, too."

"Lies," she echoes / I can hear in her voice she still believes them.

I used to be the same way / believed everything I heard / she said / I was four / seven / ten—didn't know not to. What I did know was that I'd never win so there was little point in trying / stayed in my lane / on the bypass / slow lane only / don't draw attention / be small.

It's sad watching Mama be small / she's so big on the inside.

BEANO

One time, I talked to her dog for an hour. It was one of the nights when I plugged all my outlets with chewing gum. The dog went from one outlet to the other and tried to lick the gum off. It presented a problem.

I wanted the dog to stop yapping all the time. It never shut up. However, I didn't want to electrocute the dog, either. That would be bad.

We talked. Her name is Beano, so I said, "Hey, Beano, how come you bark so much?"

She answered, "Because everybody in this house is deaf."

"Deaf how?" I asked.

"You know," she answered.

I knew / I know / it's just when it's happening to you, you don't say anything because your barking is all used up on yourself.

Weekend in #7 Minor

YELLING

Daddy is yelling in the northeast corridor. Mama's yelling back. I don't know what language they're speaking / sounds like Disappointment / needs more angel cards. Pretend-Saturday brunch has been postponed / I've eaten two sloppy ham-and-cheese sandwiches while standing next to the fridge.

"I have to get out of here," Richard says from the darkened living room.

I thought I was alone. Richard doesn't see me jump / probably didn't see me eat potato chips out of my hand like a horse.

"I can't stand it anymore," he says.

"They always yelled," I say. "Maybe yelling will lead to actual talking about stuff."

Richard grumbles.

I lean in the doorway facing the living room.

Something creepy is happening to Richard. He's a black hole. "Want me to open the curtains?" I ask.

"No."

"Are you okay?"

"Sure," he says.

"So what's the problem? Why do you have to get out of here?" I ask.

"She's not in rehab," Richard says.

"So?"

"She escaped rehab, and now she's back here trying to move in."

"Or," I say, "the biggest liar maniac you know called you and acted like a big maniac liar."

He shakes his head in frustration / rifles can only shoot if someone's in charge.

I say, "You're smarter than this."

He looks up at me / holes for eyes. "You really don't know anything about this family, do you? At your age, you really don't, I guess."

The age card / Fear and Anger.

"What happened with Giselle Masterson and you when she was thirteen?"

"What?" he says.

"I said, what happened with Giselle Ma—"

"I heard what you said. Who told you that? Mama? She told you, didn't she?"

"I thought everyone knew," I say.

"You don't know anything," he says. He gets up. Walks right for me / turns left and scurries west into the passage. I hear him crying / skipping rope / yelling in Portuguese a few minutes later. I probably should have handled that better.

GARBAGE DISPOSAL

I see Richard leave in the car a pretend–half hour later. Mama and Daddy are a crashing surf of yelling and crying and stomping. I'm still hungry so I grab a bowl from the cabinet / pour in some corn flakes and milk.

Richard's book is on the table. *Lolita*. I pick it up and shove it in the garbage disposal / don't turn on the garbage disposal / leave the job to whoever gets to the sink next. Finish eating / put Richard's book back on the table. I rinse my bowl and leave it in the sink / am speaking the language of Mild Disrespect.

As I navigate the skinny passageway on the way to my room, I don't expect a collision at the intersection with the main hallway.

"Out of my way," Mama says.

Daddy is behind her, weighed down by his toolbelt. He stops to hammer in a single clip to keep some wires from drooping.

$$x \text{ equals I wish more than anything to stop time.}$$

I know what's about to happen / psychic or experienced / you choose. I'm frozen with something I can't describe / truth / white as yogurt. There is no white petal on Plutchik's flower, same as there isn't a black petal for Richard. Black is the mixture of everything. White is the absence of everything / I can't move my legs. The longer Mama stares at me, the less I can speak / move / survive / to understand anything is to understand energy.

Daddy catches up. He says, "Concordia, I love you. Why can you not just come home?"

"Don't call me," Mama answers, pushes me gently back toward the kitchen, and then instant as current, she's out the door.

I look at Daddy, who is now shuffling through the conduit backward, claw hammer out. The noise of his work is infuriating. My insides are worms / snakes / on fire.

PLUTCHIK'S TAKE-OUT MENU

Anger. You will eat Anger until you become a plutonium bomb. You will seethe / your heart will beat out of your chest / your table settings will rearrange themselves / you will not go home / you will eat subpar pizza / you will walk nighttime sidewalks in circles / you will not pull nails / you will give up / this explanation will do.

SUNDAY VISITOR

The car is in the driveway / ours, not Mama's. No one is awake. Dawn is just poking through the dark sky. As I climb into the me-shaped hole, I wonder if Daddy made any progress on the passage to the attic. He needs to change the air-conditioning filter before it gets hot, but he forgot how to get there from here / too many layers of safety.

I sleep / dream / am woken up by my phone chiming from wherever I left it.

From Carrie. *Can I come over?* / we still don't take any visitors.

I debate not writing back at all, but I remember yesterday. And Mama. And Richard.

Text me when you get here. DO NOT ring the doorbell.

Carrie texts five minutes later / arrives on the front porch as I'm navigating the passage between #7, my room, and #1, the foyer. In our house, you pronounce that properly. Even if we did take visitors, Daddy wouldn't let you past it if you called it a FOY-er.

I open the door and tell her to follow me. Once I climb into the plywood and head back toward box #7, she whispers, "Holy shit."

I whisper back, "This is the normal part."

We get to my room and she looks around / looks back at me. "What the fuck is this?"

Before I can answer and tell her everything I've wanted to tell her since fifth grade, the intercom squeaks and Daddy says lunch is ready. His Sunday lunches are more like weekday dinners. It's how they eat where he's from. Big lunches, small dinners.

I answer back, "Carrie is here. Can she come, too?"

It takes Daddy two full Trojan-claps to answer. "Yes, of course. She is most welcome!"

BRATWURST TACOS

Everyone should know that bratwurst tacos are a bad idea. Even Daddy. The two words shouldn't fall anywhere near each other in a cookbook.

"These are surprisingly good," Richard says. He's sitting in his usual seat. I'm sitting in my usual seat. Carrie is sitting in one of the spare chairs. He won't look at either of us.

"Thank you, son."

"Delicious!" Carrie says. She's on her second taco / not lying.

I nod, a blob of sour cream dropping from my taco.

"Homemade tortilla," Daddy says. "Make anything taste good."

Carrie finishes her second taco and sits, watching us. Carrie was never taught to eat slowly and mindfully. Most people weren't. I am glad for Daddy and the stability he's given us in the parts of life that no one ever talks about. I guess Mama did that too / I should give her credit but I don't / she's not here / this explanation will do.

"What's that?" Carrie asks. She points to the nest of boxes around the switch outside the kitchen doorway.

Richard, Daddy, and I freeze.

"It looks like you're building one of those mazes for mice," she says. "But human-sized."

Daddy's face twists. Not angry, but embarrassed.

"That's a switch that needed to be covered up," I say. "And the rest is my dad's project. He's an artist."

Daddy looks satisfied.

"I didn't know that about you, Mr. Becker," she says. "How cool."

"Yes, cool," Daddy says.

Richard pushes his chair from the table suddenly / says, "I have to study." He leaves his plate unrinsed in the sink and skulks into the southwest passage.

Daddy gets up and starts to do dishes and when Carrie and I go to help, he says, "Go! Go! Visitors do not have chores!" like he's some kind of grandmother. He adds, "Truda, I need supplies and will go to hardware store after. Will your friend be staying for the day?"

Carrie and I didn't work out a specific plan, so I just say yes and figure I can change my answer later. When we get back to my room:

"You live in a really weird house," Carrie says.

"With really weird people," I say.

"I don't even know what to say. I came over because I was pissed about my parents fighting all weekend, but this is—it's—I don't know."

"Shocking?" I ask.

"Different."

I watch Daddy leave the front door and get into the car from my window. I grab my crowbar. "I have about a half hour of chores I have to do. Can you chill for a bit?"

"Sure?" she says, then looks at the crowbar. "Why are you holding that?"

"I have to pull nails," I say. "It's part of Daddy's art. I take out the nails he puts in when he's not here. He says it's a representation of life in America." I put on my best Daddy voice. "I am common laborer / crowbar represents oppressive capitalist government and culture."

She laughs. I take off to box #4, Daddy's bedroom. I hook the crowbar under nail heads, pull them, put them in my sweatshirt pocket, then wind my way back through the living room #2 / and the foyer #1, pulling as many as I can.

The whole time I burp bratwurst tacos. I know Daddy is burping, too, over at the hardware store. He feels shame, I bet. It's our main emotion. Shame isn't on Plutchik's Clock by name, but it's / I'm / wedged somewhere between Sadness and Disgust.

When I get to my room, Carrie says, "I don't know what's going on around here, but I don't like it." She's serious, too. "Are you okay? The vibes are weird. The whole thing is weird and Richard was a silent creep at lunch and I'm worried about you."

I start to cry / not used to mothering.

She hands me tissues. I say I'm just tired / we bond over parental arguing / *Don't call me.* But then she won't let it go.

"So our parents are a mess. Okay. So what's this all about? It's not art."

I want to argue with her about art / remember that Carrie has known me since fifth grade when she moved here.

"Does my sister still call you?" I ask.

"I finally blocked her a few months ago."

"Why?"

"She sent me a bunch of dick pics. She's not right, you know?"

"I know," I say.

"Is this about Richard?" she asks. "You know—the—thing?"

"It's so much bigger," I say through sobs. "So much bigger."

I tell her what I know. Which isn't much.

WHAT CARRIE DOESN'T KNOW ABOUT HER FRIEND

In this house there are four switches.

Energy flows to them

/

they are the energy.

They have names, not numbers.

Daddy is the switch.

Mama is the switch.

Richard is the switch.

I am the switch.

on / off.

on / off.

Someone else runs the energy

even though we no longer

pay the bill.

She asks me why. I tell her there is never a why. Not to the punches / slaps / not to the kicks under the kitchen table. Not to the setups or insults or lies or rumors. That poor bird / our poor family. She has stabbed us all with a screwdriver / watches us squirm / none of us have mouths anymore.

She asks me why again.

"Probably jealousy," I say through snot. "That's what Mama always said, anyway."

Dear Truda, Your legs are too skinny and I hate you for being born.

ERIS

The crying has stopped. The stories of betrayals / tricks. I assert my ability to see it for what it is / AFT3RMATH. "But Richard is still getting phone calls, and my mom, too."

"Why don't they block her?"

"Richard says he can't because she might need him in an emergency."

"Sounds sketch," she says, "but maybe Richard's sketch all around."

"Do you know how the Trojan War started?" I ask her.

"Not really, no," she answers. "You'd think they'd teach us that considering the whole Trojan thing."

"There's a goddess of strife and chaos. Eris. She started the Trojan War by getting three other goddesses to fight over who was the prettiest."

"That's dumb."

"It's mythology," I say.

"Your point?"

"The Roman goddess of peace is Concordia. That's my mom. In Greek, that's Harmonia."

"And Eris is?"

"Discordia is the opposite goddess in Roman, and Eris is her equivalent in Greek."

"And she starts wars."

"She starts everything. All strife. All discord."

"Damn. That's deep."

"Before my mom moved out, my sister tried to frame my dad in some love affair story she made up. None of it worked. Daddy doesn't do that kind of stuff. But she even got a bra and showed it to Mama and said she found it in Daddy's car."

Carrie shifts suddenly. Sits up. "When was this?"

"Last spring, I think."

"Red bra with orange lace around it?"

"I didn't see it."

"It was my bra," Carrie says. "She gave me ten bucks for it."

"Eris," I say.

"Damn," Carrie says.

When she leaves for home, she gives me the nicest hug / almost nice enough to trust that she's really my friend / she blocked my sister from her phone / didn't sell her a bra on purpose.

THIRD SHIFT

Sunday night while everyone is sleeping, I remove more nails than I ever have before. I can't stop. My crowbar has incentive. Collapse the house / collapse the family / collapse the idea that everything is fine because look around / everything is not fine.

I wish I could stop time and take all these nails out right now / make the house seem normal by morning. I keep wishing to stop time—since a long time ago / to rest.

x equals *Freeze! Nobody move!*
x equals *Wouldn't that be cool?*

I'm in my track uniform. I don't know why I put it on / was looking for strength / am trying to get used to it. I'm under the foyer, standing on a pile of boxes in the basement to get at the nails. Something is different / I don't usually glow / it's not the glowing.

Everything is silent. Not quiet. Silent. The nails make themselves known by groaning out of their holds / cry for help. I can't hear the fan in the heating ducts. I can't hear the timer for the water heater ticking. I consider that I might even be dreaming.

Pull nails / pull nails / pull nails. I push myself because I've never been this tired from just pulling nails. It feels like I've been doing this forever. I've sweat through my uniform and my hair. The bag I strapped around my shoulder is heavy with steel.

I must be getting better at this / that's all.

I go upstairs for a glass of water.

It takes four paper towels to wipe off my face and neck—I'm that soaked. I smell like the ocean / not on a good day. I stand at the sink and look out the window at the streetlights and gulp. Something is in the front lawn.

Richard.

He's just standing there.

x equals me tapping on the kitchen window to get his attention.

x equals Richard doesn't move.

It's raining. Richard hates getting wet.

I go out the front door and something is wrong.

The rain isn't falling as much as it's there / stuck midair / there is no wind.

"Richard?" I'm six feet from him. He's got the car keys in his right hand, aimed toward the driver's side door.

I walk right up to him. He's frozen in time. The trees are frozen. The rain is frozen. The scene is silent. Not a drop of anything here.

I have stopped time / am walking around in time / to understand anything is to understand energy.

I touch his arm. It's chilly. I wonder how long he's been here / a mannequin. I reach around to his back pocket for his phone. I put in his passcode / it opens to N3WCLOCK.

N3WCLOCK says it's 2:03 a.m. This is impossible. I started at pretend–one in the morning and have been pulling nails for at least three hours. I've already emptied my nail bag twice / too many to count.

The snakes inside my body return. I worry about Richard. I shake him a bit, try to wake him up or push him out of whatever it is that's happening. I look to the sky and to the ground and I marvel the lack of energy when everything has stopped / check my hands / still glowing.

I feel responsible / the game I'm playing with Daddy and his nails now has consequences. I go back inside, get my crowbar and pull a few in the kitchen. Nothing changes. I stop in front of the sink again and close my eyes and breathe and tell time to start again.

Nothing changes.

I beg it / nothing changes.

I *broke the world*, I think. Richard will be forever frozen in our front yard like a middle-of-the-night lawn jockey. Forever feels so real when it's happening inside my head.

I see one of Daddy's hammers on the living room side table. I pick it up and find a nail.

For a minute, I think of how great it would be to live in this quiet world. No one would bother me / I would be lonely / wouldn't matter if Mama never came home / kept her word. I look back at Richard frozen, standing in the grass / the nail in my hand.

Hammer it in / rain hits the roof / wind whooshes.

I go back outside.

"Where are you going?" I ask Richard.

He looks at the keys in his hand / back at me.

"How long have you been standing there?"

"I'm not standing here. I'm sneaking out. Don't tell Dad."

He gets into the car and backs out the driveway in neutral, lights off, then heads up the street toward town.

By the time I get back to box #7 / put my crowbar away / lock my door, the house is making its normal noises again / breathing.

I go to bed and dream of nothing / dream of the javelin / arrow stuck in time.

Potluck

THE PLAN

Len has edited his documentary. He said it took him all weekend. I'm glad someone was thinking about the plan while I was busy playing my part at home / the plywood carnival.

Nigel isn't here, but the culinary teacher is apologetically cleaning up from a faculty breakfast potluck. The smells of hard-boiled eggs and bacon permeate the room.

I get up and play pretend–Solution Time. "What do we do when we feel Fear?" I have my marker, my whiteboard, and my notes.

"Adrenaline," Eric says. "It makes us jumpy. Anxious. Fight or flight."

"I always get a weird taste in my mouth," Len offers. "Sweating."

By the time the culinary teacher leaves ten minutes later, the board is covered in words and phrases.

Adrenaline, jumpy, anxious, fight or flight, weird taste, sweating, can't breathe, shaking, wanting to leave wherever you are, unsafe, angry about it (is that disgust?), hide under the covers, running from nothing and then hide under covers, goose bumps, heart beating out of chest, overcautious, paranoid. I didn't add any of my own words or phrases about Fear. It's the water in my fishbowl / AFT3RMATH.

I take a picture of the board for my notes, and the five of us gather around Len's laptop.

"Came in at four minutes but I still want to cut it to three," he says.

We watch, mesmerized, for all four. Len has footage of Nigel drinking gin in his car, talking inappropriately to three cheerleader girls, and more than one classroom tirade—ours included, with a close-up of Nigel spitting that shit at Eric about his dad / failing us all.

"How'd you get the shots of other Solution Time teams? You were here the whole time," Eric says.

"We're a network," Len says.

"A network of Lens," Carrie says. "That's both terrifying and soothing."

"Are you going to post it publicly or send it to the school board?" I ask.

"I haven't decided yet," Len says.

Nigel will definitely get fired. It's only a matter of when / before next Monday—thesis-statement Monday—would be ideal.

MAKE NOISE

We train in the weight room for an hour after two slow laps around the track and then go back to the field. Coach Aimee hands me three javs.

"Your form is . . . something we should work on," she says.

"Is that what I'm judged on?"

She slides me a look like I'm taxing / I probably am taxing.

Picture Coach Aimee trying to teach me how to throw like the other throwers. I trip twice. Go over the line. I throw too high and too wide. The jav may as well be a yardstick. I can't get it past the thirty-yard mark and it wobbles out of control / leaves me behind. Coach Aimee looks oddly pleased at this. She knows I'm nervous.

"Can't I just throw it the way I throw it?" I ask.

"I can't stop you," she says.

I throw / a projectile vomit / about 160 feet.

I leave the field an irresponsible-to-form, yet capable javelin thrower.

In a weird twist, the whole team is summoned to the gym. I lag back to see what's going on. Everyone grabs a yoga mat as we walk in, so I grab one, too.

We stretch and then Coach Aimee's new student teacher leads us in a guided meditation / I've been doing this with Psych Team for months now.

"Really blow that breath out of your mouth!" she says. "Make noise!"

My teammates exhale with confidence. They moan and growl and make noises like dying machines. I can only manage to exhale calmly. I want to growl, but I can't. I just think about Richard last night, stuck in the arrow / sneaking out / Mama said something about a girlfriend. I don't really meditate at all / am afraid what will happen if I do.

When I finally get up / last one / the student teacher says, "Don't you feel so much more ready for tomorrow? Good luck!"

I feel worse about everything. But mostly that I didn't hear a single word Coach Aimee said at the end and I hope I didn't miss anything important.

I explain this to Carrie as she drives me home.

"Did I miss anything about report time or anything? I zoned out."

"Nope. All you have to do tomorrow is remember your uniform, spikes, track suit, and anything to keep you warm. It's going to be a chilly one!"

Carrie is like my track dad or something / compensating for the plywood maze. I can't tell her that I can stop time / can't tell anyone.

POPCORN

Daddy is working in box #3 / the kitchen. Everything is disorga-
nized / there is a ladder. I can see his boot above me between two
beams where the light fixture used to be.

"Where are the snacks?" I ask the ceiling.

"In box on table. Make sure no sweets. Not good before
meetup," he says. I grab two bags of plain popcorn—Daddy air-
pops it once a week and bags it with metallic red twisty ties—and
say I need a shower and I'll be in for dinner whenever he needs me.

"Wait. Wait," he says / climbs down / goes to the intercom
unit and asks Richard, "Come to kitchen, please."

Richard arrives, a mechanical pencil still in his hand. He looks
tired / agitated. He fires me a look like I tattled on him for sneaking out last night. I launch a shrug in reply / try to shrug in Portuguese so he likes me again.

"We have family meeting after dinner," Daddy says.

Richard and I nod.

"We have problems," Daddy says.

Richard and I nod again. Can't deny that.

"We are sick family who needs doctor," Daddy says. "So I bring
doctor. Carmichael is coming today!"

Daddy doesn't have any friends except for Carmichael. Carmichael was always imaginary to me because I only ever heard him
on the phone.

FAMILY MEETINGS

We haven't had one since Don't call me. Mama always ran the
meetings—sometimes about homework and permission slips /
sometimes about problems. The problem meetings usually failed /

impossible to have a family meeting with an assortment of bombs / this explanation will do.

CARMICHAEL

When Carmichael comes, he crawls through the passages, admires the conduit, and he compliments Daddy on his work. They act like brothers who were separated by the Berlin Wall. There is warmth. Carmichael can correct Daddy's English and tell him he has a chunk of oregano stuck to his front tooth. They drink wine and talk in the kitchen and cook while Richard and I sit, as instructed, in box #2 / the living room waiting for dinner.

"Carmichael is not a doctor," Richard says.

"Maybe he's an exorcist."

Richard sighs / safety off but he can't grasp the trigger / his hands are fists.

"Why are you so mad all the time?" I ask.

Richard gives a look like I should know.

"How are classes going?" I ask, pointing to the book he's been carrying around.

"Pretty good."

"Did Mama talk to you this weekend?" I ask.

"Did she talk to you?"

"Yeah," I answer.

"Is she coming back?"

"I don't know," I say. "I think so?"

Daddy and Carmichael make noise in the kitchen. Water / metal spoons / laughter.

"Why were you up so late last night?" Richard asks.

"I could ask you the same thing."

"Are you spying on me?" he asks.

"Why would I spy on you?" I say.

He doesn't answer / looks out the window / the window is steamed up from whatever is happening in the kitchen.

He's so jumpy I can't tell what he's going to do next / I wish he had a hobby or something he likes to do / something that would make the energy sit still. I have the jav / Daddy has the boxes / maybe Richard goes to a midnight macramé class or yoga / doubt it.

CARBOHYDRATES

"Eat! Eat!" Daddy says. "You need carbohydrates to perform well at your meetup."

The pile of spaghetti on my plate is large and I am hungry enough to eat all of it. Daddy's homemade marinara sauce is the best / Richard always picks out chunks of tomato.

Carmichael hands me two pieces of garlic bread and says, "Eat," and then turns his attention to Richard. "Tell us about your college, son."

I eat half the spaghetti mound as Richard tells a story about his literature class and how he didn't expect to like it / about his math teacher and how tall she is / about his biology professor who doesn't believe in evolution. That one makes Daddy and Carmichael laugh.

"This is American education we came here for, yes, Carmichael?"

Carmichael just shakes his head.

"May I have more bread please?" I ask.

Daddy puts the entire basket in front of me.

Richard tells another community college story, and Daddy and

Carmichael explain that they come from places where education is serious. "No pom-pom cheerleaders," Carmichael says. "It was study and more study and even then, to go to university?"

What Carmichael means is that it was impossible.

Richard says, "Community college isn't university like you know it."

"It is better than poke in eye with burnt stick," Carmichael says.

Daddy laughs and I conquer the rest of my spaghetti.

"Can any of you see that I'm glowing?" I ask.

All three of them look concerned. I hold up my hands. They're still glowing.

Richard and Daddy don't say anything but Carmichael grabs my hand and says, "You are full of energy! You are readying for a match. Of course you glow."

"Meet," I say.

"Yes, meeting," he says. "Do you have cheerleaders?"

"No," I say.

"Serious sport," he says / his eyebrows wiggle.

"I guess."

"Your father and brother will be there and will cheer you."

"I have class," Richard says. "Sorry."

There is a chasm in the conversation / no one but Carmichael can keep it going / Carmichael gives up here.

Daddy finally pushes his chair back from the table and sends Carmichael and Richard to the northwest passageway to locate the way to the air-conditioning unit, and starts doing the dishes. He hands me the tea towel and tells me to dry because, he makes a throwing motion, "Take care of hands for grip."

When we finish, Daddy pulls out his favorite teak cheeseboard / special occasion / family meeting. As he gathers hunks of cheese from the fridge, he says, "In half hour, we have meeting. Go do schoolwork."

He releases me from duty without his usual hug / he is hugging cheese / nervous.

I don't know what he has to be nervous about / everything is already fucked. That's why this is called the AFT3RMATH / things can only get better from here.

Time is moving perfectly backward. I am working toward my own birth / OR1G1N. Sometimes life moves this way / backward / birds get murdered / reclaim your own time. When you lose something, you retrace your steps / this is the same. I came home from the hospital when I was born / was misplaced at some point / am retracing my steps.

Eventually, I will become who I was supposed to become.

CHEESEBOARD

Carmichael is already sitting in Mama's green chair. I sit on the love seat under the window. The steam from dinner left drip marks / I'm still glowing / Daddy and Carmichael are too engrossed in telling jokes to each other to notice. Richard's eyes are looking brighter, but he still feels like a void / unloaded rifle / loaded rifle / you choose.

"Let's begin," Carmichael says, sitting forward.

Daddy clears his throat.

Carmichael says, "Richard, you must tell Truda what happened with that girl."

Richard sits, hands in his lap, shaking his head slightly.

"I already know the story," I say.

"It's not what you think," Richard says. "I never even really talked to her. That's all rumors."

All of us stare at him.

I say, "She's a year younger than I am. And was in seventh grade."

"She didn't look it," he says. "But all we did was text and send memes to each other. Nothing else happened."

"Jesus," I whisper. I want to freeze time like last night / give Richard an escape / I don't know why / there is no escape from this / she didn't look it.

Daddy says, "If your brother had done more than this, we would have allowed girl's brother to beat him."

"Jesus," I whisper again. No wonder I'm Paleolithic. I live among cavemen. "Why are you telling me all this?" I ask.

"You made mention of the girl at dinner this week," Daddy says. "You said she refused to talk."

"Her name is Giselle," I say.

Carmichael asks, "Has she been able to live normal life?"

My face twists. "Um, yeah. She seems to be living just fine?"

"Good," Carmichael says.

"This is ridiculous," Richard says. He gets up and starts pacing in the middle of the room. "Mama shows up on Friday night, you guys live it up for a night and then she disappears again and you have me in family meeting court defending shit that didn't even happen three years ago?"

"If nothing happened, why is it such a big deal?" I ask.

Carmichael smiles at me.

Richard hangs his head.

Daddy says, "The father of the girl came to our door. He said your brother was pedophile. Mama and I had explain to him about your sister and what she does. If not for that, Richard would have many broken bones."

Sister.

"And yet you still talk to her," I say to Richard.

"I'm her only family."

"She talks to Mama, too," I say.

The room goes quiet. We are missing Mama / not missing Mama / ignoring the accusation / the word pedophile.

"Why did Mama leave again?" Richard asks.

"Women are shadows," Carmichael says.

Richard raises his voice / faces Daddy directly. "Why did she leave in the first place? You can't keep a job? You can't—" Richard circles his hands. "You can't do whatever it is that keeps a wife happy? What was so wrong?"

I say, "Everything was wrong."

"It was not your father," Carmichael says.

Daddy lowers his head. Richard sits back down on the couch.

x equals *You had nothing to do with this.*
x equals *Your father is devastated, but it's for the best.*

Daddy goes to the kitchen and comes back with glasses of wine for him and Carmichael, the cheese plate, and a book.

The book is a book his grandfather gave him / not in English. He pages through quickly, past many annotations and underlined sections, until he gets to the passage he's looking for.

Daddy turns to Richard. "You want to know why Connie left and

I will tell you. Before this, you listen to Truda. You purchase thing you did. How say—own it? You own thing you did to that girl."

"Her name is Giselle," I say.

Richard says, "I didn't do anything. It was all a lie. You know who did it."

Sister / no one says her name / superstition.

"Then why do you still talk to her every week?" I ask.

"She knows things we don't," Richard answers.

"She makes them up. That's how she knows them," I say.

"She told me Giselle was sixteen."

"Which proves my point."

Daddy continues to hold his spot on the page in his book with his index finger. He is watching us talk / table tennis. He and Carmichael are smiling oddly at each other when they meet eyes.

Carmichael asks Daddy, "You did not do what I told you, no?"

Daddy's Carmichael-smile disappears. He nods.

"Richard, you should no longer be in contact with your sister," Carmichael says.

"I'm twenty-one years old and can be in contact with who I want."

Daddy says, "You do not listen. You never did. I disconnect phone tomorrow."

Carmichael says, "You told me this was already done."

Daddy says nothing.

Carmichael says, "You never lied to me before."

Daddy says nothing.

"You are too quiet with these children," Carmichael says. "You have made your life so much harder."

Daddy pulls a nail out of his pocket and looks around for where he left his hammer. Before he can get off the couch to retrieve it, the living room / box #2 begins to turn clockwise and his book falls from his lap.

We get down on the floor / instinct / try to hold our gravitational footing. The love seat slides toward the corner, Mama's chair nearly levels Carmichael on its way to the same place.

The standing lamp falls over / bulb breaks / Richard catches the embroidered wall hanging Mama made as it unlatches from its hooks on the west wall. Daddy races to get two other, larger art pieces from the same wall so they don't fall on our heads. A forgotten wood carving plunks down and hits Carmichael on the shoulder. The noises from around the house sound like a boat going under. Creaking / bending / breaking / churning. We grab for stability. I cling to the door frame. Richard to the windowsill, and Daddy and Carmichael try to act like men who know what to do / push the couch over / slide the coffee table to safety / eat cheese. Finally, the rotation stops after a full ninety-degree turn. None of us gets up.

Someone has picked up Daddy's plywood maze / turned it on its side. Richard and I are sitting on top of a Matisse print on the east wall / now floor, with a perfectly laid-out cheeseboard on our laps. Daddy and Carmichael crawl into the kitchen to clean up spilled wine.

Part Two

1NCID3NT / EV3NT

RETAIL THERAPY

More than half the people at my school have a N3WATCH now. I'm sure they're on time for stuff, but that's not why they have them. They were on time before the watch / another fashion accessory / were just scared.

When people don't know when something is going to end—or start again, in this case—they go a little cracked. Everything feels like forever. Energy trapped in the unknown / like the fire under Centralia, Pennsylvania. Except, in Centralia, everyone knew the energy was a noxious mine fire burning for decades and they eventually had to move away. There is no moving away from a fold in time and space.

Except for N3WATCH / makes the fire go out / only in your mind.

THE ANOMALIES

In late pretend-February, Ms. Moreland, our social sciences and history teacher, made us research the effects that the stoppage of time had on our society. One of the mini-assignments included three links to articles about people who were suddenly able to do extraordinary things. Anomalies: a fifth grader in Illinois had recently solved an impossible PhD math equation / a girl named Jennifer in Nebraska had figured out how to fly. The third article was of most interest to me / more important than flying. It was about a doctor who could heal fractured bones without eight weeks in a cast—he would just touch the break and it would heal.

I found the restoration narrative encouraging.

I remembered Beano and her claim that everyone in my house was deaf. She wasn't being literal / talking dogs are not usually literal / we can all hear just fine. Yet restoration was necessary and pulling nails was my part in that.

It was the way in which I learned how to rest inside a fold in time and space / move inside an unmoving arrow / heal inside the AFT3RMATH.

By the time we decided to destroy Nigel, stretches on Plutchik's Clock became more natural. It didn't have to be a certain time of day or hour I put aside, I could simply feel my feelings when they happened / not be ashamed to have them / move on with my life.

It's a matter of survival / same as purging sister / always moving forward.

Robert Plutchik didn't just invent his wheel and then walk away from it. His whole life was a study of emotion and evolution. How we evolved as emotional beings. How we survived *because* of our emotions.

Paleolithic / cavemen had the same emotions we do / instinct.

Fight or flight is a well-known and accepted reaction to Fear. It has saved many lives. But what we overlook when we ignore talking about emotions in day-to-day life is that there is survival in Joy or Anger. In all of our emotions / if we listen.

x equals how Disgust is a reaction to poison.
x equals vomiting until the poison is gone.

Plutchik didn't stop there. In his decades of study, he found he was able to predict the socioeconomic future of a family line based on how they deal with emotions / trauma. I'm no Robert Plutchik, but from the look of my house, lies and silence can destroy a family's future more effectively than a hurricane can.

GRAVITY

Last night was a night of learning for all of us. Mostly we learned not to walk on the exposed walls / old floor without knowing where the wall studs are. This was a concern only in the rooms or halls that are missing full plywood safety boxing. My foot went clear through from the living room to the corridor / two sheets of drywall / never meant to bear weight. Richard tried using his skis to walk around / they got caught up in the conduit. Carmichael continued to crawl for the most part, as he solved plumbing problems all over the house.

When I said good night and went to my room, everything was a ninety-degree mess. GPS: If I face the window at the front of the house, the floor is now the wall to my right / the ceiling, the wall to my left / my doorway is two and a half feet high / six and a half feet wide / nothing comes with directions.

Before bed, I did basic cleanup. Bed upright, mattress back on it, comforter and sheets and pillows. I found my teddy bear. I found my phone charger and an outlet on the wall-now-floor and plugged in my phone.

Today is waking up to a pile of my own furniture and clothing, my yellow comforter wrapped around me. I remember / the house turned. I get my backpack from under my desk, now on its side, and gather the things Carrie told me to bring. Uniform, track suit, spikes, and I toss in a small fleece blanket because she said it would be cold.

I'm unsure where my me-shaped hole will lead me this morning. Maybe to school, maybe to the sky.

I go to the kitchen where Daddy and Carmichael had put the table in the right place, picked up the fridge, and got it working. The sink is disconnected and on the floor. My lunch is on the table like always and no one is around.

I leave a note on the table. *Happy Birthday, Daddy! See you at the meet!* ♥

It turns out my me-shaped hole leads to the sky, but I go out anyway. Climb down the roof sideways, and then have to jump to get to the grass in the backyard.

Carrie sees me walking through the parking lot at school. "Bad morning?"

I look down at myself. There's grass in my hair and the arm of my sweatshirt has dirt on it.

SURPRISE SURVIVAL

Psych Team talks about survival. How we must destroy Nigel's world with Len's video before he knows it's about to fall apart / can retaliate.

I find Plutchik's graph on survival sequences. "Look. You find an obstacle or an enemy. It makes you Angry. You destroy the enemy."

"This class is my enemy," Carrie says.

"And so we shall destroy it," Len says. "Before the end of the week."

"But not today," Carrie says. "It's track day. Tru and I have to focus."

Eric asks Carrie something about track and I zone out and study Plutchik's survival sequence chart for an answer to how I feel about my house being turned sideways. There's no way to tell Carrie— even though she was at my house two days ago. She wouldn't even believe it. I skim the emotions. Joy / Trust / Fear / Oh.

I find Plutchik's survival explanation for Surprise:

Unexpected event → questioning what it is → stop → gain time to orient.

I stare at the words. *Stop. Gain time to orient.* Like Zeno's arrow.

No other survival issues connected to Plutchik's emotion wheel have anything to do with time / this is a personal breakthrough. I know what's wrong with time.

Time was surprised.

So it just stopped in order to orient.

Or someone stopped it.

I don't tell anyone.

Special things happen during phenomena like this. Like our house becoming a bingo spinner. Surprise!

UNIFORM II

The top is still tight across my chest and I feel conscious about my boobs and how people can see them when I run / bounce / throw.

I'm worried my ass looks big / shorts are tight.

I'm worried about Daddy. He doesn't know what to do at American high school stadiums. The one time I took him to a football game, he talked about the lights so much he made all the people around us mad with his electricity / halogen logic. And today he'll be alone because Mama and Carmichael and Richard are busy.

He will not know to buy me a candygram.

He will not know that the concession stand is open and selling his favorite candy: Good & Plenty. It's the only candy he eats.

Today, he is fifty-one years old. My mother is forty-six. Neither of them knows how far a javelin is usually thrown by high school girls.

I think of the medal I might get.

I think of how maybe it will be a day to celebrate and maybe people will be happy for me. I have no idea why this goes through my mind as I walk to the field judges alongside Giselle Masterson and the other two girls. They probably don't care whether people are happy for them or not.

JAVELIN CHECK

They make sure it's the right weight and the right style. They don't even look at me—no idea I'm about to make them doubt their sanity. Or mine. Or whatever else is about to happen.

It's my favorite jav: teal with purple highlights. It's my favorite weight: 600g. It's my favorite day: Tuesday. It's my favorite weather: cold and overcast.

HOLD / DECK / UP

I.   On Hold.
     The runners are running / jumpers are jumping and I
     thought I'd feel more self-conscious being in the middle
     of the field but it's all so busy. Makes me wonder why I
     never went to a track meet before / went surfing before /
     did anything I haven't done yet before.

I want to try new things.

I want time to start moving again so we don't always have to spend our free time thinking about solutions.

I don't even think there's a problem.

II. On Deck.

I don't look up at the bleacher people, cheering on their running / jumping / throwing kids. I don't look up at all, really. Not ever.

I've always had trouble with eye contact / attention / praise. I have echoism. Google that if you want. I'll wait.

III. Up.

Watch me throw, now.

ANGRY

That's what the main field judge is—angry. She thinks I'm messing with her head when I tell her I shouldn't throw unless the track and beyond it is clear. She rolls her eyes like I'm making a joke / the runners who know me watch as they round the far turn.

"Throw. Or be disqualified."

So I throw.

The field judge thinks I'm cheating the minute I throw because of course she does. I've been building this throw for a week / month / year / my whole life.

She inspects my arm and hand as the two other judges try to measure my throw but can't because their tape isn't long enough. She asks the assistant judge to retrieve my javelin, which is on the opposite side of the track, which means I just threw at least two hundred and thirty feet (just short of the women's world record, NBD).

She disqualifies the first throw due to "technical difficulties," and that's when Coach Turner shows up and argues. She won't budge. Coach Turner eventually says, "Technical difficulties, my ass. The only technical difficulty here is inside your head."

I stare at the grass, mostly. Someone gives my jav back to me. I stand there looking at it / the grass / then the crowd. Daddy is standing and clapping. Still. Three or more minutes since my throw.

No one has told him to sit down.

SECOND OF THREE

On hold. Giselle Masterson throws a really nice 123'. Her form makes my form look like it's dry heaving. She has javelin DNA. I have DNA that can't stop expanding via plywood, conduit, and energy.

On deck. Kelly throws a wobbly 95'. Best throw today, so she should be happy, but she's not. She will not be happy until she is Giselle Masterson.

Up.

The field judge looks at me like I'm about to rob her house / murder her dog.

I walk back to the grass beyond the toe board—I call it the runway like I'm an airplane because I am about to fly.

NEVER TURN YOUR BACK TO THE THROWER

This is an actual rule in the rule book / I read the rule book fifty times / it's why I was so freaked out about field judges. Now, I am more freaked out by field judges because this one refuses to understand the Paleolithic nature of me and this spear.

She probably relies on N3WCLOCK, too.

Anyway, the field judge has her back to me, which means she's the only one breaking rules today. Not me.

I sprint, step sideways three times, hop, and throw. Feet off the ground, I launch it toward the woods at the edge of our stadium. It won't make it all the way there, but it's nice to think about what would happen if it did. The jav lands even farther than my first throw.

They have prepared themselves with two measuring tapes. One judge stands where the jav landed and holds a stick with the zero part of the tape attached, another judge waits to see how far that judge gets until her tape runs out. The second judge has another tape. He puts his stick at the end of her tape and walks back to the toe board.

Math gets involved.

I'm standing here. Coach Turner and Coach Aimee are here. Giselle, Kelly, and Petra (finally remembered her name) are back in the warm-up area, spike-throwing their javs to stay in the zone.

The second judge walks toward the toe board with his tape extended nearly the full distance.

"Two fifty-seven," he says.

"Two fifty-seven?" the field judge asks.

He looks at her crooked. "Yeah."

She waves at the judge still out beyond the throwing area, holding the stick at the place where the javelin landed. "Two fifty-seven is impossible. That's world-record stuff, Carl. Come on. This is ridiculous."

"You're a freshman?" she asks me.

"Junior."

"Did you just move here? Don't remember you from last year," she says.

Coach Turner says, "This isn't an interrogation. Tru throws better than anyone I ever saw. Well—farther, anyway."

"We can't mark two fifty-seven," she says.

"Why not?"

"It's impossible." Two other judges have come by to nod in agreement.

I am surrounded by skeptics while time has stopped and there is no solution. The same people will go to church on Sunday and pray to an invisible man. They will check their N3 WATCH to make sure they aren't late for the sermon. They will go to the smorgasbord afterward and eat maple syrup that is not actually maple syrup, but artificially-flavored sugar liquid on their not-real pancakes.

"I am not impossible. Let me throw it again," I say.

Coach Turner puts his index finger to his lips for me to shut up. He is arguing for me / I will only fuck it up. Coach Aimee is surprisingly bitchy on my behalf. I'm glad she's consistent, at least.

THREE

On hold, Kelly tells me that Giselle Masterson has written a letter to the PIAA / state athletic board and reported me for using performance-enhancing drugs. There is a 75 percent chance Kelly could be lying about this.

Giselle throws a tired 105'.

On deck, while Kelly throws, I ask Giselle.

"Did you really report me for using drugs?"

She looks startled. "Who told you that?"

We both look at Kelly as she throws a decent 88'.

Giselle shrugs. "Javelin throwing in my family is sacred," she says. "Like Jesus-sacred."

"So you think I'm taking drugs?"

"I don't know," she says.

"I'm not taking drugs," I say.

"You're up."

"I know. But this throw won't count—even if I push it all the way to Ohio."

"You should probably just quit," she says.

WHAT YOU DON'T KNOW ABOUT THE TALENT SHOW

One time I could sing.
I would stand in the backyard
when we lived at the townhouse
and I would breathe right
like the teacher taught me.
Hand on my diaphragm.
I was in third grade
and I loved Diana Ross
because Mama loves Diana Ross.
Talent show /
signed up secret, decided
lying was better than
an audience with my family inside of it.
Sister was in fifth grade
signed up to do lip sync with her friends /
saw my name /
said at the dinner table
Did you hear Truda is going to sing at the talent show?

The way she said it / pressed the button
the button under the table /
the button born in her hand /
she pressed it and
they all laughed at me until I told the chorus teacher
to take me off the program /
out of chorus.
Mama: *You'll only make a fool of yourself.*
Richard: *Trust me. You don't want to do that at your age.*
Daddy: *You will be better off.*
The button / switch works on everyone.
Everyone.

TWO NINETY

I look into the stands before I throw and Daddy is still standing, his right hand acting as a visor even though there is no bright sun. He's watching, making sure I'm not making a fool of myself / am better off than a third grader singing "Baby Love."

I roll my neck. Roll my shoulders. Throw one last time.

I hadn't heard it before because I wasn't listening. This is my first track meet. I am the last contestant—the way they wasted time arguing. My whole team—Carrie, Kevin, and John and all the sprinters and that kid who pole vaults and that high jumper who might make it to states again, and even Giselle Masterson, Kelly, and Petra—are standing on / around the bleachers and yelling my name. *Go Tru! Throw it, Tru! Go Becker!*

I'm not used to this / can't make out if they mean to support me or burn me later under the scoreboard as an example.

My run is good / hops are good / form is good. I stop way

short of the toe board because going over it scares me. My release is clean and I feel like maybe my dry-heave form is simply mine and I don't need to be like Giselle-javelin-DNA.

The jav lands over the track again, this time beyond the shot-put area.

All the coaches are there. I hear Turner say that he's called the AD. I don't know what the AD is so I just ask the judge if I can go yet because my team is cheering and I want to be part of that even though I have no idea how to be cheered for.

Daddy is still standing. He is wiping his cheeks—either sweating or crying. Daddy doesn't sweat.

"Stay," Coach Turner says. "We're fighting for this one."

I stay.

I keep my eye on Daddy. He's walking down, now, toward the team.

The field judge comes back with a distance. Two ninety / two hundred and ninety feet / impossible. They all argue.

"You'll mark it," Coach Turner says.

The field judge finally marks it in the book. I have officially thrown two hundred and ninety feet. I have no idea what this means, really. A man with graying hair and a Trojans track jacket extends his hand to me and says, "Congratulations, kid. You just set a new world record."

AD means Athletic Director. I know this because he tells me as he puts his arm around my shoulder, grins wildly, and asks Coach Turner to take a picture of us together. Then Coach Turner wants one, so they switch places. Coach Aimee is already over with the team.

I thank the field judges and then walk by myself to the bleachers.

Daddy has been given / has purchased an official Trojan Track
and Field windbreaker and a baseball cap. He walks out to meet
me and hugs me / holds me by the shoulders and smiles / hugs
me again.

"Happy birthday," I say.

"Thank you."

"You look like an American," I say, nodding at his new hat.

"I feel like man of the world," he answers.

"How does that feel?" I ask.

"Very proud of you," he says.

Everything goes silent / familiar silent. I look at the bleachers
/ everyone is frozen. Daddy is frozen in a proud half hug with me.
Coach Turner and the AD are frozen, walking behind me, one of
them laughing. Coach Aimee is frozen with a bitchy look on her
face while she talks to Giselle Masterson. I didn't want time to stop
/ don't know who stopped it / hope it's not random like sneezing.

I slide out of Daddy's frozen hug. Like a me-shaped hole.

I walk around the frozen landscape / Zeno's Claymation / I am
the only thing with motion. All else is in the arrow.

"Am I proud?" I ask.

I do four handsprings across the grass. I am proud of handsprings.

I sing the song that helped me memorize all the state capitals.
I am proud of knowing my state capitals.

x equals how I'm lying about being proud.
x equals how I'm not lying about being proud.

I can't grasp that I'm on the track team and that I just broke a world record. I know it happened, but I know I can't claim it as my own. It's complicated / Diana Ross.

I walk back to Daddy and slip into his hug again. My arms around him / time moves again / I answer his question.

"I'm proud to be your daughter."

It was the only thing I could think of.

Daddy and I break the hug / he is no longer smiling. I am high-fived and fist-bumped and Kevin almost gives me a chest bump he's so pumped but he realizes at the last minute that he can't do that.

"DUDE! TWO NINETY! THAT'S SICK!"

"SO SICK!" Kelly says.

"IT'S GUINNESS BOOK OF WORLD RECORDS!"

I suddenly just want to be with Daddy / do not deserve anyone being this happy for me / need to be in a room by myself.

"Truda Becker, please report to the field judge," comes over the PA system and the AD, Coach Turner, Daddy, and I end up standing on the track with the head field judge and her cell phone on speaker while the rest of the team trickles out of the stadium.

The field judge says the person on the phone is a state track official.

"We've had complaints," the phone speaker says. "Of drugs."

The AD says, "Is there a drug that would make a kid this age and size throw two hundred and ninety feet? Because if there is one, I have yet to hear of it."

"We've had complaints," the speaker says again.

"I don't take any drugs," I say.

"You can file all you want, and we can test her if we have to," the AD says, "but as of right now, a world record was set on my district's track and I'm calling the goddamn papers."

Heels are dug in. Even the other team's coaches are fighting for me and my Paleolithic. One says, "I watched every damn throw, and it was real as anything."

Daddy takes me gently by the arm and walks me toward where the celebration was happening only a few minutes ago. The track team has gone back to their locker rooms / families and fans have gone back to their warm cars. Daddy has me tucked into his new windbreaker and we walk up the stairs out of the stadium.

"I'll meet you right there." I point to where Carrie usually picks me up outside the locker room. "In five minutes."

"We need to celebrate," he says. I picture going out to McDonald's with other kids my age. He continues, "I will make a meringue!"

OPEN EYES

Mama is waiting on the front porch when Daddy and I pull into the driveway.

"I don't even know how to get into my own house!" she says.

"You do not live here," Daddy says. This is a bad sign.

"I just came from the most enlightening therapy appointment of my life," she says. "We have to talk." She winks at me, but has no idea how bad her timing is / ironic for psychics, I know.

"Truda just broke world record," Daddy says. When he says it, he smooths down his new gear and adjusts his hat.

"I don't have a lot of time. The dog's in the car," she says.

On cue, the dog starts yapping.

Daddy says, "I do not think you heard me. Your beautiful, talented daughter broke world record today. WORLD RECORD!"

I don't hear her reply / this explanation will do / because Richard arrives in the driveway via the side window of box #11. He walks directly to me and hugs me. Won't let go. It starts to scare me. Until he leans down and whispers, "I have the keys to the car. We have to get out of here."

I can't tell when to trust Richard / this is the time to trust Richard.

Our parents stand in the driveway talking. Mama says something about how her therapist *opened her eyes* and Richard and I scoot closer and closer to the car until we can jump in, start it, and Richard peels rubber as he races down the street.

"She'll never leave us now," Richard says. He's breathing like he just ran the steeplechase.

"Wouldn't be a bad thing," I say. "As long as the fucking dog doesn't come back with her."

"Not the mother. The sister."

"Oh."

"They're a team," Richard says.

I DISAGREE

Richard's imagination fires rubber bullets. I don't disagree with him out loud just yet / little sisters follow rules.

First, I hand him a test.

"I broke the world record today," I say.

"That's impossible."

"I'm serious. In javelin."

Richard's frown digs deeper between his eyebrows. "Where?"

"At the meet."

"You broke the world record today?"

"Yes. I did."

"I don't know how to feel about that," he says.

Stop time. Car frozen / Richard frozen / I step out the passenger's door even though we are driving sixty miles per hour. I walk around the car / get to Richard's side / open the door. I inspect his head.

Inside his head there are no feelings about my breaking a world record. He's telling the truth. Someone took all his nice words / pride. Left him with confusion and yardwork at Karen's place / an imaginary mother-daughter team / no AFT3RMATH. Rubber bullets sound bouncy, but they actually blind and kill people all the time.

I get back in the car and start time again.

"They're not a team," I say. "She's just lying to you."

"It doesn't make any sense," Richard says. "Mama knew we needed her—Daddy can't do anything but hammer shit and Carmichael is just a clone."

"Mama's not a bad person and she tried her best," I say. "And our sister is lying because she's a liar. That's all. That's all it's ever been."

"Why?" he asks.

"Because she can? She likes attention? She hates us? Whatever. Who cares? She's gone for good and yet you let her call you! Why?"

"In case of emergencies?"

"Bullshit."

"She's blood," he says.

"Bullshit."

He looks at me / is out of answers.

I say, "She knows your secrets. That's why."

I am the stopper / starter of time.

I am the thrower of spears / energy.

I am the siren / I will tell you.

I will deconstruct the boxes and one day we will all be free.

Paparazzi

RESCUE

We can't park anywhere near our house. We only went to the next town and circled back. Richard was saving me from my mother. And I didn't need saving because she had just had her eyes opened in therapy. And now we're trying to find a place to park but there are TV vans everywhere. Just like in the movies.

I don't want to talk to anyone.

But Daddy. Daddy in his new school-colored windbreaker coat is talking to these people. Lights / microphones / Mama's car is gone.

"We have to save him," I say to Richard.

A horn honks behind us.

Richard stops the car and I stop time. I weave through all the frozen reporters and camerapeople and lights and gawkers and neighbors and I take Daddy by the hand and pull him stumbling toward the car.

I start time once we're all safe inside.

"We're going out to eat!" I say.

"To celebrate Tru's world record," Richard says.

Daddy is speechless in the back seat / maybe an effect of moving through frozen time / tongue needs to catch up.

I say, "The meringue will have to wait."

NATIONAL TEENAGE HERO

Richard asks why Mama left again and Daddy says, "TV vans make her nervous. She will be back later."

"Back for how long?" Richard asks.

"I want her back forever," I say.

"Me too," Daddy says.

"But not with the dog," Richard says.

"We have worked out new marital contract," Daddy says. "No leaving or yelling or making bad days."

"Sounds good to me," I say.

Richard doesn't say anything else but for once, he isn't scowling about it / might be breaking free. He decides we should go a few towns away so no one recognizes me. We go to a classic diner well after the dinner rush and ask for a booth in the back. We sit and I take off my jacket and put it on the back of my chair.

"You're still in your uniform," Richard says.

"We are Trojans!" Daddy says, pointing at my sweats and his windbreaker.

I look down and see that the only thing I've changed is my shoes. I am technically still wearing record-breaking clothes. "We are Trojans," I say. I make Daddy fist-bump. He hates new things, but he fist-bumps me.

"I wish I could have seen it," Richard says.

"It was incredible, son. Your sister has magic in the arm."

I nod at this. I do have magic in my arm. I can now stop time / make it rest like Zeno's arrow / move inside it.

Richard says, "God, I'm hungry," pulls his smartphone out of his back pocket and opens N3WCLOCK and says, "It's eight forty."

Daddy and I look at the menus. I decide on a Belgian waffle.

Richard does things on his phone while the waitress comes with small glasses of ice water and utensils-in-a-napkin bunches.

Daddy asks her, "Is anything here homemade?"

"All our pies and cakes. Fresh every morning."

I add, "You can't go wrong with breakfast."

Richard reads on his phone / aims his rifle. "It says here that you didn't really set a world record."

"Can I get youse started with something to drink?"

"Water is fine," I say.

"Coffee," Richard says.

"She set world record," Daddy says. "Put the fucking machine away or I will make cook deep-fry it."

Richard freezes. The waitress freezes. Daddy is breathing and blinking and he relaxes his shoulders or else I'd think time stopped again.

"I would like two farm-fresh eggs poached and rye toast, please."

"Any meat with that?"

"No meat," Daddy says.

"I'll have the Belgian waffle, please—with just butter and syrup."

"Powdered sugar?"

"Yes, please. Oh. And a chocolate milkshake," I say.

Richard says, "I'm going to wait in the car."

"Order food, Richard," Daddy says.

"You can't make me eat."

I say, "We're celebrating. Please. Order food."

Richard looks from his phone to me, and then back at his phone. "Why can't I tell you what I'm learning? People are fighting about this. Online! Right now! We're missing it. I want to at least see the TV. You're my sister. I want to set them straight. They probably never even held a javelin, let alone threw one."

"Are you that girl?" the waitress asks. She adds, "You are! You're her!"

I say, "My brother wants two eggs over easy, French toast, and bacon."

Richard nods. "And a small orange juice."

Daddy says, "She is the girl, but please we eat without interruption."

"Yes, sir," she says. She looks back at me. "You're a national teenage hero!"

"She is magic," Daddy says.

The waitress stops at the front counter and says something to the woman there. The woman then turns up the volume on the TV. The athletic director and Coach Turner are live outside Trojan stadium.

"So talk to me a bit about the future of Truda Becker," the reporter guy says.

"I've already gotten calls from all the big track schools. They all want her," the athletic director says. "But I tell 'em we get to keep her another year because she's only a junior!"

"Olympics 2024 are a given," Coach Turner says. "Such a natural talent."

"We're very proud of all our Trojans, but it has to be said—you don't get an athlete like this very often."

"What do you think about the rumors of drug enhancement?" the reporter asks.

The athletic director starts to say the thing he said at the track three hours ago—about how if there's a drug that makes my arm magic, then he's yet to hear of it, but I don't want to hear it again / play this game / be a national teenage hero.

I stop time and move the chess pieces around.

x equals *Freeze! Step away from the pie counter.*

First thing I do is take Richard's phone from him / zip it into Daddy's windbreaker pocket. Then I unplug the TV in the diner / scramble the cable box by hitting the reset button. Back in the kitchen, the cook is frozen scraping off his grill and humming along with the radio. I unplug the radio / take the radio and put it in the trash can in the ladies bathroom. I stop there and look at myself in the mirror.

To understand anything is to understand energy.

The energy of stopped time weighs a ton and my shoulders hurt from holding the diner / town / world in place. But hot damn, I do look good in this uniform. Go Trojans.

EGGS

I return to the table and start time again. Richard stares at his hands. The waitress tells me from behind the counter that she's working on my chocolate shake. Daddy says, "I do not believe eggs will be farm fresh."

I laugh. Richard laughs / seems to not care where his phone went. He says, "So weird, but my hands are tingling."

We ignore him. The woman behind the pie counter is gesturing angrily at the TV with its remote, saying something in Greek.

"I'm glad Turner said that thing about you having natural

talent," Richard says, still shaking the pins and needles out of his hands. "That must be nice."

"They were nice," I say.

"No. I mean having a natural talent for something," he says.

"You have a natural talent for school," I say.

"It's school. Memorization and regurgitation. That's not like being able to set a new world record."

"I don't know. It's too soon to tell," I say.

Daddy listens but only repeats himself when he speaks. "I do not believe eggs will be farm fresh."

"It will all be delicious," I say.

Richard says, "Yeah."

"So how do we get home so I don't have to talk to any of those reporters?" I ask.

Daddy frowns. "Why do you not want talk to reporters? You are magical girl who broke world record."

"I'm shy," I say.

Daddy laughs. "Shy! Truda! You have never been shy! You talk to everyone since you were little girl." Sister hated that / everything about me. Always younger / more adorable / talking to strangers.

"Never in front of cameras. And not after revealing that I'm a freak."

Both of them look at me in a way that hurts my feelings.

MASLOW'S DINNER MENU

At the very least, you need the egg yolks to be yellow. These eggs are feeble / barely more than blond. Daddy raises his eyebrows and he stares. Poached eggs depend a lot on yolk color.

"Not farm fresh," he says to the waitress.

"Where else would eggs come from, sweetheart?" she says.

Daddy cocks his head. Smiles. *Sweetheart* will stick with him for days. He shakes on too much pepper and keeps looking around the diner to avoid seeing what he's eating.

Sweetheart.

Daddy is a sweetheart. Mama is, too, only you walked in at the wrong time / during her confusion / a half-psychic yo-yo. So is Richard, only you walked in while he's still keeping secrets. And so am I. I'm a sweetheart. Paleolithic spear right through your heart—I love you that much, stranger. We are all sweethearts until you ask sister / hates sweethearts / thinks they're suckers.

Picture Maslow's pyramid of human needs. Gently place four sweethearts / suckers into the triangle. Now. Toss in a maniac. Cook for eighteen years. Open the Maslow-oven-door. What's for dinner? / plywood and boxes and conduit and a switch that no one will touch. What's for dinner? / a pack of sweethearts who can't figure out what they did wrong. They didn't do anything wrong.

DESSERT

"Any dessert for youse?"

"Why do you say that?" Daddy asks.

"Our pies and cakes. They're delicious."

"You say *youse*. You have American education. You know this is not word in English," he says. "Even I know this not word in English!"

The waitress looks hurt.

"No dessert, thanks," I say. "We have to head home."

Daddy says, "Sweetheart, I was not trying to hurt feelings. You will find man easier if you have dignity with your words. That is what I mean."

"Who says I don't got a man?" she says.

I sympathize with Daddy. He is literal / gullible. He thought she really thought he was a sweetheart. He is a sweetheart. Only sweethearts correct your grammar and care about you finding a man, right?

I say, "I'm sorry. My dad is from somewhere else. He's not great with . . ."

She slaps our check down on the table and goes back to the kitchen.

CREEK

Knee-deep in freezing cold water / the creek behind our house / Richard's idea. Daddy lies to reporters in front of the house while we sneak into the back. Our shoes dry as we wind through miles of twisted ninety-degree plywood and conduit to the kitchen, where there's a note from my sister on the table.

Dear Truda,

I hate you for being born.

Kidding. There's no note. Instead, there's residue of the note.

Carmichael arrives, pliers and wrench in his hands / crawls under the half-installed sink.

I hear Daddy on the front lawn saying, "Truda has no drugs. That is not her style."

I can't make out what the questions are. But Richard turns on the TV, now propped against the living room wall / former floor and I can see Daddy / hear Daddy saying, "I do not know what you mean about this time anomaly. Truda is national teenage hero."

Crowbar

LOCKDOWN

Daddy gets in through the him-shaped hole / front door and declares an emergency.

Fight or flight / lock all doors / find a buddy. Carmichael has moved to the basement to fix more plumbing. There are brown stains forming in every corner of every box / trickles of liquid / a faint smell of sewage.

Daddy, Richard, and I decide it's best to turn off the TV. Richard has located his phone in Daddy's windbreaker pocket / dives into it instead.

Daddy gets a glass of wine / uses a paper cup. This is out of the ordinary but they didn't serve wine at the diner, so he's just probably superstitious. He offers one to Richard and Richard says yes.

"Can I have one?" I ask.

"No."

I don't even like the smell of the stuff / no idea why I asked / was probably testing my boundaries. Mama once said that the job of being a parent was to be the walls of a swimming pool. Your children will push off of you, and your job is to be steady concrete. None of us expected so much structural damage from the explosions.

"All window shutters down," Daddy says. He has a large, gray, industrial remote control unit on his lap. There is a switch for this. He flips it and the windows shutter closed.

"I am electrifying perimeter," he says.

I say, "Hold on, what?"

"How do they say it here? Get off lawn?"

"Get off MY lawn," Richard corrects.

"Yes. Get off MY lawn," Daddy says, flips a switch and because of the window armor, I can't see anything that happens outside. I hope he's not accidentally frying anyone. That would look bad.

We sit for a while in silence.

Daddy says, "I do not understand why you will not talk to them. You did wonderful thing."

I say, "People are already saying I take drugs. You can't do anything good in the world without someone complaining, I guess. Plus, it's not like I worked hard at it."

"You practice every day," Daddy says.

"For three weeks. No one can throw a two ninety after three weeks. Olympians don't throw that after lifetimes of training," I say.

This makes Richard look up from his phone. The two of them stare at me. I suppose I'm being awfully matter-of-fact. They're only finding out who I am / Paleolithic / powerful. I've known for a while / not as affected as either of them by the bird / screwdriver / almost immune now.

"I'm a freak of nature," I say.

"Stop saying that word," Daddy says.

"Yeah," Richard says. "You're not a freak."

"Well, then, what am I?"

Carmichael yells from the west passageway bathroom / box #8, "You are extraordinary. Compliment, not insult!"

"Call it what you want, but I don't have a good feeling about this."

Carmichael arrives, now armed with an acetylene torch and two small copper fittings that he's jingling in his left hand like bells. "That is natural," he says. "When did you ever have good feeling about anything you have done?"

The residue of the note—it's asbestos, not a virus / immunity is impossible once you inhale. Only thing to do is remove it / then heal your fiber-sliced lungs.

"Richard, I need you to find small eyeglass screwdriver I borrowed you," Daddy says. "It is in your bedroom."

When Richard leaves, Daddy leans to me and says, "You have always been extraordinary girl. You grew in garden overgrown with weeds and disease."

"Listen to him," Carmichael says.

I say, "I never did anything great before. I see no proof of being extraordinary."

"Today is proof enough," Carmichael says. "Celebrate these moments, Truda. They do not come often in life."

"It still doesn't answer why. Like—why? Why now? Why me?"

Daddy and Carmichael have no answers.

Richard returns with the eyeglass screwdriver and sits back on the couch.

Last week I thought it was because of all the things I never did—all that energy was stored up. But now I think it's because of my crowbar. I think the universe is rewarding me for dismantling Fear. The switch—I will be the one to pull it. It's just like telling the truth / making your own yogurt / throwing a spear / Paleolithic.

Daddy seems satisfied as he hears car engines starting and people talking loudly outside and cars driving away.

"You're sure you didn't electrocute anyone?" I ask.

Daddy laughs and yells, "Get off my dammit lawn!"

LOCKOUT

I'm in the garage area with my crowbar / dismantling Fear. It's got to be past one in the morning N3WCLOCK time, and someone is banging on the shuttered front door.

I hear yapping.

I walk to the garage door, and I peek through the window shutter slats. The yapping is Mama's dog. The banging is Mama.

I run through the house to find Daddy. I accidentally stomp through the wall / floor plasterboard in the hallway. By the time I'm in the main house, I run right into him.

"Ouch!"

"Sorry."

He turns on the light.

"Is that a crowbar?" he asks.

"It's not a chocolate cake," I say.

"Was that you—" he's about to ask me if I was making the noise, but right then, Mama starts banging again.

"It's Mama."

We stand in the hallway, me in my sweats and sock feet, holding a crowbar, him in his brown bathrobe and barefoot, holding the large remote control unit.

"I am taking her back," Daddy says, "but not with dog." He marches toward the front door / him-shaped hole / goes outside. Through the open door, I see that there are no TV vans / fried reporters on our dammit lawn.

I go to my room to put my crowbar away and look around / relive the living room scene yesterday. Carmichael, us, the TV, coffee table, couch, and the Tiffany lamp all flopping over like we're in a slow-motion clothes dryer.

I only had one dresser and it's jammed into the corner now, on
its side. The mirror is cracked and the drawers are a mix of out and
in and one of them is on the floor / crooked / broken.

I check my phone, where I find a text from Carrie saying she'll
pick me up for school tomorrow. I crawl to the kitchen for a snack.
Richard is there, drinking milk from the carton. "Do you even
sleep?" he asks.

"For about four hours, yes."

"And you break world records."

"Sure."

"Excelente," he says, Portuguese pronunciation on point.
"What was all that noise?"

"He's going to let Mama move back in as long as she doesn't
bring the dog."

"Sim!" Richard laughs. "Sim, sim, sim!" He is playing an agree-
able part in a Brazilian movie. I wish I knew enough to play along
/ didn't live inside his Brazilian movie.

Since we ate at the diner and then had to get rid of the reporters, I haven't had time to look around. The kitchen is a war zone.
Carmichael has put half-inch plywood on the now-floor so none
of us fall through the walls / now-floor. The old linoleum floor
is now the wall where the stove was. The countertops are vertical.
Half the cabinets are missing / the ones on the now-ceiling ripped
a lot of drywall with them / the rest are sideways / duct-taped
shut. I can't even make sense of it.

"This place is crazy," I say.

The front door opens and closes. Daddy arrives with Mama
next to him / her eyes take in the battlefield / mouth says nothing.

They're holding hands. "We must replace all locks before tomorrow," Daddy says.

He and Mama walk, arms around each other's waists, toward the passage that leads to their bedroom. Richard points to the hole I made in the living room wall yesterday and tells me, "*Tampões de ouvido* means 'earplugs' in Portuguese."

LOCKSMITH

The next morning, Daddy has new keys laid out on the kitchen table for me and Richard. Richard is still asleep. I'm going to school, where I have no idea what to expect. World-record breaker / drug taker / freak / who knows what trouble I will get into for being Paleolithic / honest / yogurt today.

"You must change the keys now," he says.

"You'll be home when I get home. I'll do it then. I'll be late," I say.

"Just take old keys off and put new on, please," he says.

I do as he says. He makes me put every last one on my key chain and then I go out to wait for Carrie. Across the street, there are two news vans and a car. I didn't expect the news people to even have interest anymore. Daddy must have turned off the electrified perimeter because I'm walking right down the driveway and feel fine.

I don't have the N3WCLOCK app and I can't tell if I'm late or early, but I feel like I'm waiting way too long for Carrie, and maybe because of TV people, she didn't stop. I hate being late for school—though technically we're all early for school because it's still June 23, 2020.

When I got outside, I put my tampões de ouvido back in, so I can only see the TV people mouthing questions at me. I can't just look at them while they strain to be the one I hear the loudest, so I look up at the sky. I cloudbust. I see a rabbit and a spaceship—the 1960s flying saucer kind. I see a small toy train. And then I see a cloud couch. I see her, aged thirteen, arms outstretched, saying, "Hey, come up here and I'll tickle your feet." I see me at ten years old, floating from the floor to the couch / giggling. I see a cloud pillow. I see her hit me with it / pillow fight / feel two punches right in my crotch.

x equals how they weren't punches, exactly.

x equals how punches don't last this long.

Even in the clouds, it hurts.

Carrie has clearly gone to school without me.

I walk in to Mama and Daddy having sex in the hallway outside the kitchen.

"I'm walking to school," I say as I turn back toward the door. "I was late for Carrie."

My first step after turning around lands off-stud and my foot goes through some exposed plasterboard between the foyer and the kitchen. I pull it out and as I walk to school, I brush the white dust off my right leg and drag my sneaker through long grass / nothing fully removes the residue.

Residue

INTERVIEWS

"I didn't do it on purpose," Carrie says.

I wait.

"My mom told me there would be reporters all over the place," she says. "Frankly, I'm surprised you came to school at all. Because—"

Because of the swarm coming at me right now. Coach Turner, the athletic director, and the principal, who says, "We notified all your teachers. Don't worry."

"Worry about?" I ask.

"Homework or class or tests or any of that."

"Your grades are looking great," Coach Turner says / thumbs up.

Last time I checked, I was barely holding the B average.

"I don't want to be on TV," I say.

"It's just one interview," the principal says. "You'll be done in no time."

We walk through the main office and to the principal's corner office. "The crew is set up in there." She looks me up and down and turns to Coach Turner. "Carl, do you have official track gear she can wear?"

"I can get Aimee to grab her extras," Coach Turner answers.

He and the athletic director sit first while I wait for word on track gear. The principal and I stand and listen to the interview through the door.

"Some internet followers have written their concerns about

what happened yesterday," the guy says. "Some people think she could be from another species."

"Another species!" The athletic director laughs.

"Extraordinary? Yes, she is. Extraterrestrial, no," Turner says.

"Let's not forget that athletes like this come around every few years," the AD says. "Bobby Road scored twenty-five hundred points on the basketball court five years ago and nobody ever implied he was an alien."

"I didn't mean to imply she's an alien," the guy says. "Our viewers. They have—um—wild imaginations, I guess. But you have to admit, this is a bit of an anomaly."

"I saw it the first time I watched her throw. Was it out of the ordinary that she could throw the way she did yesterday? Not really. First day she probably hit one twenty."

"Is that normal for someone's first throw?" the guy asks.

Coach Turner says, "It's normal for Truda's first throw."

The principal's walkie-talkie clicks and she walks away from the door, and I hear Coach Aimee say "I left the warm-ups on my desk with a pair of decent Nikes."

I nod to the principal and head to the locker room to change / have always wanted a pair of Nikes.

PALEOLITHIC ALIEN INVASION

It's difficult to care about someone who is asking stupid questions. Daddy has raised me all wrong. The news guy starts with boring kindergarten stuff. How far did you throw again? / 290 / and how old are you? / 16.

Then he asks, "Do you think this is you throwing the javelin, or do you think something else is happening?"

I answer, "Do you think this is you asking this question right now or is something else happening?"

He struggles / the Nikes fit perfectly.

"Let me start again," he says.

I sit up straight in my chair like Daddy is watching.

"How did it feel to break the world record?"

I smile. "It felt good. Like I found my place in the world. In high school. I'm finally good at something."

He laughs. "I'm sure you were good at other things before now."

"Not really, no. Not like this."

"It *would* be an understatement to say this is being *good* at something. You're clearly exceptional at javelin, right?" he says.

"Clearly," I say.

He's still flustered / I can't tell why / there is a nugget of plaster in my sock from the foyer wall-floor / seeing my parents naked.

"Have you heard of the others?" he asks.

"I don't listen to popular music," I say.

"Oh. Sorry. I mean the other kids like you?"

"Did you know that one of our throwers has an Olympian father? Same event. Javelin. She's got beautiful form."

"So you're a real team player?"

"I like to think I am," I say.

He flusters again, then asks me a few questions about college and the Olympics / I give him stock answers as if Coach Turner took over my audio. I know what he's trying to do—he's trying to make me into the girl who can fly or the kid who does raucous math / he's trying to make me agree / alien headlines. I ask if I can be released for class / they remove the microphone and wires from inside the Trojan track suit / I am free.

FOREVER FRIENDS

I've changed back into my regular sweats. Coach Aimee said I could keep the Nikes, so I did / of course I did.

Daddy didn't pack me lunch today on account of him having sex all night. He'd make me call it *lovemaking* if he was here. Whatever. I don't have lunch.

By the time I make it through the lunch line, I've been talked at a hundred times. I have no idea what anyone said to me. It was all some sort of static. I land at the table and flop myself into my chair.

There's a weird quiet, so I fill the gap. "My parents were having sex in the hallway this morning," I say.

Carrie says, "I'm glad someone's getting laid."

They laugh and then the table goes quiet again as I look at the disgusting lunch I just bought. Two prepackaged bowls of room-temperature flavored yogurt that tastes like bathroom cleaner. I look back up and they're all looking at me, smiling.

I think I've done something wrong until Len says, "I'm so fucking proud of you."

He gets up and makes a motion for a hug. It's the best hug I ever got. When I turn around, Eric is standing and he wants one, too. And Ellie. And then Carrie, who already hugged me yesterday in the locker room, but does it anyway.

"You look—different," Ellie says.

"You look scared," Carrie says.

"I *am* scared," I say. Pure Plutchik Green.

"Of what?" Ellie asks.

"What does *forever* mean now?" I ask.

They look at me.

"Remember *friends forever*? Like—last week? What if it turns out your forever friend is a freak and people think she might be an alien?"

"Alien?" Eric says.

"Yeah, you're totally an alien," Carrie says.

"You're not a freak," Ellie says.

"The reporter pretty much asked if I was an alien, not kidding," I say.

"I kinda want to kick someone's ass right now," Len says.

"I feel like everyone's looking at me."

"They are," Carrie says. "Isn't that why you threw so far? So everyone would look?"

I'm stunned.

I never thought Carrie would be this untrustworthy. She Googled echoism when I told her / knows my buttons.

I glance at Eric, whose eyes are now swimming in his phone. Ellie is silent, but watching.

Len says, "That's rude." He laughs because he's trying to give Carrie a Carrie-shaped hole, but she's not using it.

"Anyway," I say. "Thanks for the hugs."

I freeze time / the cafeteria / get up / walk out. I only start time again after I've cried for fifteen pretend-minutes in the bathroom.

PRACTICE / NOT PRACTICE

Carrie is finally apologetic on our walk from chemistry to the locker room.

Finally apologetic = factory-made low-fat artificially-flavored
lunch yogurt

"I think I'm pissed because you're really this good," she says.
"I mean—look at you."

THE SWITCH II
What is the switch?
   I mean—look at you.

WHAT YOU DON'T KNOW ABOUT THE SWITCH
It wasn't in the house
when we moved here
not precision-machine work
unlevel / poorly mounted.

Now that I think of it—
Looks just like the box
Daddy used during
yesterday's emergency.

Now that I think of it—
Time is on strike
because it was tired
of how much of it
we've wasted
on bitchy bullshit.

WHAT YOU DON'T KNOW ABOUT THE SWITCH II

I am not the most coordinated
not the most graceful
not a fan of cardio.
I mean—look at me.

I am not the smartest / no
detective. I can see
something wrong /
not name it.

There are no forever friends /
something is wrong.

Carrie keeps walking to the locker room but I slip left into the
main office and ask if I can speak with the athletic director.
"He's long gone, hun," the secretary says.
I'm quitting track team / right now / tone it down / look at me.

Castle / Moat

PLUTCHIK'S FAMILY DINNER MENU

Mama is delirious with therapy in the driveway. She's spinning and her psychic skirt is the wheel that drives her machine. It whirs.

When I arrive home early and unsweaty, she doesn't notice or ask why. It's Daddy, from the roof where he's replacing a shingle, who says, "Why are you not at your meetup practice?"

"I just . . . couldn't today," I say. I hold back tears / am sadder than ever / look at me.

"Tomorrow we will see mayor and get picture taken!" he says. "It is good, Truda! So good!" He's not trying to cheer me up / is legitimately this excited to meet the mayor.

I say to Mama, "I wish I could just avoid people for, like, two weeks solid."

"Healthy boundaries are everything," she says / I'm not a client.

I wish I could talk to her / she's too busy spinning. I wish I could trust her / she's too busy spinning. I try my me-shaped hole, just in case, and it works.

I yell down to Mama, "Thank Daddy for fixing this!" but then I look around. Everything is in piles again. My bedroom is completely upside down. Ceiling where the floor should be. Floor where the ceiling should be. All the socket holes look like aliens, with a third eye on their foreheads. Mouths erased. No more "Ooo!"

The blinds on my windows hang under the windows, two of them hanging only by one side. The ceiling-mounted light fixture is flattened and the light bulb inside has shattered. My bed is upturned again, the dresser is lying facedown. Part of box #7's plywood is curling away from the wall / losing structural integrity with each turn / slow leak brown liquid.

I sit on a pile of clothing / dirty / clean / who would know. I think about the structural integrity of everything. Time has stopped. Minutes no longer jog along reminding people that they're wasting their lives. None of us is wasting any time. Not even Len, who is probably at home masturbating to twentieth-century hard rock. Not even me, who is skipping track practice.

I've seen it everywhere / how the integrity breaks. Nigel— Solution Time passive / aggressive. Richard—still not owning what he did / almost did / thought about doing. My parents— how they fought / the things they used to say.

That's your fault—not telling him enough about girls.

You could have also told things about girls.

Integrity.

A rifle must be loaded with the right rounds. It must be cleaned and oiled / requires care / upkeep.

A missile launcher must have missiles to launch. Study the trajectory / useless without guidance / the jav shed.

Bombs just explode / this explanation will do.

Fathers just build protective layers / this explanation will do.

Mothers—mothers are the glue that keeps all the pieces in place / the walls of swimming pools / unless they leave / this explanation will do.

The partially collapsed passageway to box #3 / kitchen is limiting when upside down. There are wires hanging everywhere / free from conduit. Extension cords and fat, gray ten-square. If it rained in here now, we could all be like the moles in Daddy's electrified lawn.

He is mashing potatoes while kneeling. The fridge is upright again but the stove has been disconnected. The electric roaster oven we usually only use for holiday roasts is on the floor next to him, steam billowing from it / no exhaust fan / the windows are dripping with sweat.

There are two five-gallon buckets where the sink should be. The sink is in the backyard now / look out the living room window / along with two toilets, the water heater, a bathtub, and the chest freezer where Daddy stored his blanched vegetables.

The kitchen table has been moved to the living room ceiling / floor with two eight-by-four sheets of thick plywood so it doesn't fall through the ceiling plasterboard. It is, for the first time ever, set for only four people / this is a miracle / a shame / I don't know what it is / probably depends on who you ask.

"Why did the house turn?" I ask. No one answers.

"Can I do anything to help?" I say.

Daddy says, "Your mother has made her meatloaf!"

My mother's meatloaf is like eating damp ground socks / clean socks so it's not awful / socks with oregano and too many bread crumbs.

"Where's your brother?" Mama asks.

I go to the southwest conduit and yell his name, but when I turn around, I see that the whole time, he's been sitting in the hallway, looking at the switch, which is now upside down on the wall / not like you could tell with all the boxes.

"Oh, hey," I say.

"The house is losing structural integrity," he says.

I nod. "The house is losing structural integrity."

Mama has made a meatloaf shaped like a castle. The whole castle, fort walls and all. In the moat, there is gravy.

She places the platter in the middle of the table / has used fresh parsley as hedgerows and bushes. Some of the parsley is limp where it surrendered to the gravy.

"This is our castle," she says. "And tonight we start putting it right."

"We start with moat," Daddy says.

He plops mashed potatoes on all of our plates from a pot that's still hot from the barbeque grill / licked with charred black. For each of us, he makes a hole in the middle with his wooden spoon.

While he does this, Mama carves up the inner castle and slaps slices of wet meatloaf onto our plates / ladles gravy onto the meat / into our potato pools.

We pass around a bowl of candied carrots.

Daddy passes around a pepper grinder / nothing on his face seems to notice that this meal lacks integrity, just like everything else around us. When I look at Mama, she looks like integrity / late glue is still glue / even if her meatloaf is soggy / at least she's trying.

THE PLAN

Mama / castle queen is upright. "Richard, your father tells me that you still talk to her. He hasn't turned off your phone yet, but I will."

"I never see her or talk to her!" he says.

Mama eyes him / his cards / his aura. "Jesus, Richard, we're talking about your sister."

"Oh," he says.

Mama says, "Now that I'm back, she's not allowed within a hundred yards of this house or me or Truda. If she even walks down the sidewalk across the street, call 911."

"No police," Daddy says.

"Too late," Mama said. "Nineteen years of trying to help that girl and all I got for it was a protection order and a bad hip."

"Did you say you *and* me?" I ask.

She says, "Yes."

"Oh."

WHAT YOU DON'T KNOW ABOUT BEING A FREAK ACCIDENT

Mama never lied about it

weren't expecting you, to be honest

An unforeseen dinner guest

Daddy made extra rolls and gravy

smiled a lot / no longer had time

to learn the guitar.

I was this surprising.

Those stories you hear on gossip shows

about the lady who didn't know

she was pregnant.

but you're here for a reason

The vasectomy failed.

Mama never lied about it

you saved me from that other one

Accidental superhero age five.
Sister killing that bird with the screwdriver
Richard told me to run.
Ran so fast home to tell Mama
who couldn't save the bird.
thanks to you, she won't do it again
with extra tapioca pudding.
She did it again
again
again
not to birds / not to birds.
She became a mythical insect
so small it can crawl
into your brain and
on / off
on / off.

Richard says, "Now that you're back? Does this mean you're back?"

"I'm back," she says / I believe it / she says it with the confidence of a bear.

"When did the house turn again?" I ask.

"Why is it happening?" Richard asks.

"When and why is it happening?" I ask.

"Are we going to get a new TV?" Richard asks.

"We will sleep in the northwest area," Daddy says. "To stay safe."

Mama stays quiet / looks amused by Daddy's orders.

"My room is fine," Richard says.

"Mine, too," I say. "I can—"

"We will sleep in the northwest area," Daddy repeats, and then ladles more gravy out of Mama's moat.

BALLROOM DANCING

After dinner, Richard and I go to his room to get his stuff, like Daddy told us.

"One minute we're talking about getting protective orders, the next minute it's castles and gravy and Daddy telling us where to sleep," he says.

"He has trouble talking about things," I say.

"That's how come we're in this mess."

"Mama will change things," I say. "Trust her."

We give each other the look we've always given each other. Trust no one. There are bombs everywhere. We really can't tell who planted them—it's not like they sign the bombs.

"Karen said we should try family therapy," Richard says. "But I know he won't."

"Mama could push him. Remember the time they did ballroom dance classes?"

Sometimes, I catch Daddy dancing with himself in the kitchen. I see him spin and dip an invisible partner. I see it in Richard now / like when he was sneaking to the car in the middle of the night / something is wrong.

When you get to the AFT3RMATH, you can be yourself / maybe for the first time / maybe a reminder. For me, a first. Probably for Richard, too. For Mama and Daddy, they will have to remember. There will be an EV3NT. Mine was a world record / theirs can be whatever they want it to be. Maybe Daddy will rip down the boxes. Maybe Mama will allow herself to be one hundred percent psychic. I don't know what Richard will do / Richard is weak for reasons other than a bird / sister. His EV3NT won't happen until he stops keeping secrets.

MY PHONE IS A BOMB

As I navigate my way back to box #7, I hear my ringtone. My ringtone is an obnoxious techno dance song with elevated bass / I'm too far away to rush.

My phone is in my backpack, and it chimes with a voicemail.

The voicemail is from a major television network / three letters everyone knows. I haven't watched any of the interviews the local news stations aired and don't plan to. I don't want to be on TV. I can't imagine how a major network got my number / I'm sixteen / I skip the voicemail / press the call back button.

MY PHONE IS A BOMB II

The woman who answers is tall. I can tell from how she talks / six feet easy. I explain that I'm returning a call from this number and she asks my name and when I tell her, she says, "Oh! Hi! Hold on. Let me get Ashley."

The hold music is me rehearsing my lines. *Hi, Ashley. I don't want to be on TV. Bye / Hey, Ashley. Yeah, about the TV thing, I can't do it / I appreciate your offer, Ashley, but I'm shy and you can always interview the coaches.*

"Ashley Thompson. Is this Truda?"

"Yes, I—"

"Dude! I'm so excited to talk to you!" she says. "I have a big opportunity. I think you'll be excited."

Hey, dude, Ashley, um. "Opportunity how?" I ask.

She must be wearing headphones because I can hear her clap like my teachers used to before pitching us an assignment that none of us wanted to do. "So. 60 Minutes. Two researchers over there have been finding other kids like you. I shouldn't call you a kid. Sorry. Gray area. Anyway, they sat down with some of them and talked about their—uh—new abilities. We wanted to know if you'd be open to a fast interview."

"60 Minutes?" I used to watch 60 Minutes every Sunday with my parents—since I can remember. I even watch old episodes online for fun when I'm bored / I find relief in the opening where a stopwatch ticks as if time is really still real. They have yet to change that opening / maybe it soothes them, too.

"We would do the interview tomorrow at the latest to air on Sunday," she says.

"This Sunday?"

"Yes."

"What's the title of the story?" I ask.

60 Minutes always has great titles. "Prescription for Trouble" or "Get Me the Geeks!" or "Pot Shop."

"The Anomalies," she says.

x equals my desk thesaurus that was under a pile of clothes.

While Ashley gives reasons why this is going to be *Great! / Awesome! / Amazing!* I look through the book. The synonyms are not good. *Deviant, aberration, heretic, exception, bohemian, fanatic, flake, freak, three-dollar bill, dingbat, ding-a-ling, weirdo, teratogeny.* There are better ones. I wonder if Ashley would go for "The Punks" but I doubt it. And teratogeny is just insulting.

"So—they're making us look like freaks?" I ask.

"No! Not at all!" Ashely says. "Have you seen that kid who can fly? She's amazing! It's magical!"

"So—breaking the world record in women's javelin is magic," I say.

"It is pretty, um, extraordinary." I am quiet for so long, it seems, that Ashley has to say, "So, what do you think?"

"Yeah, I think I'm just a normal kid who's good at something. Not a freak. I can't, you know, fly. I'll have to think about it."

There's a quiet gap as if Ashley didn't expect this / most people want to be on TV / Daddy says it's the American mindset / I have a Paleolithic mindset.

"We'll have to know before tomorrow morning," she says.

"Oh."

"I kinda need to know now," she says.

"I guess you can always interview the coaches," I say.

"I don't get it," she says. "Why did you write to us and give us your number if you didn't want to do this?"

"I didn't give you my number."

"I have an email from you right here."

"I didn't send you an email."

"Huh," she says. "Well. It was really nice talking to you. I hope you'll watch the story, anyway. I know you've been a *60 Minutes* fan your whole life."

Sometimes the red hang-up button is just so obviously there for a reason. I press it / Ashley goes away / I look around my room / hear heavy rain outside / run.

Storm

MAKING DEALS WITH ENERGY

To understand anything is to understand energy.

Present tense. Here / Now.

I am your anomaly.

On the fifty-yard line / stadium around me. Soaking wet / I sit. Raindrops the size of golf balls fill the turf / half-inch-deep lotus position. I think about Plutchik's Clock and run through the colors. Can't feel a thing but cold / my project is a lie.

Lightning hits / the stadium is purple and bright. When I stand, my leg joints are sore. Walk to the shed / know the combination by heart / retrieve my jav. The whole way, I talk to the storm and make wishes.

This is not my first time.

I've been asking thunderstorms for things since I learned about Benjamin Franklin and his kite / key / probably six. To understand anything is to understand energy.

I didn't want to throw a javelin two hundred and ninety feet. I wanted to be powerful enough to change things / people giving a shit about people / find the truth. That's what I asked for. I got this instead.

x equals me never watching 60 Minutes again.

Thunder makes the aluminum bleachers shiver / tinny.

Lightning hits over by the scoreboard and I think I feel the energy in my shoes—metal spikes in a quarter inch of water.

I look up. I don't say anything, but inside my head, I'm screaming. I hold the jav up above my head like a lightning rod. I put all of my energy into my wish.

I wish to be normal Truda.

I wish to have a normal family.

I wish to be allowed structural integrity / pride.

Lightning comes right down to the field. There's a cracking sound that's impossible. A tree next to the shot-put area splits in two / explodes outward / limbs and leaves everywhere.

Three steps / bounce / throw / sprint.

Stop time / I keep flying / land in front of it / start time again.

I reach up, snatch the jav from its path, and I have completed the cycle / played catch with myself / feel completely alive.

Only it's impossible to tell anymore which of us are dead or alive / who is telling the truth or lies / we need more rest / fewer N3WATCHes.

Same as it's impossible to tell anymore who in my family is coming or going / telling the truth. Until Mama and Daddy learn how to ballroom dance again, everything steps on my toes.

My me-shaped hole is blocked when I get home. I try to push through the plywood, but it won't budge.

I use the front door.

The house has turned again, but not a full twist / diamond shape / emergency. Gravity makes us walk in corners. On corners. Straddle / navigate / struggle through valleys and rills. Daddy and Richard are in the living room, pushing as hard as they can to make the wall flat / any sane angle will do. They jump up and down as hard as they can / look like cartoon zoo gorillas. But nothing moves it.

"Truda, you are making stain on wall," Daddy says. I look down and see that I'm dripping rain onto the one place where you can still see a wall. The rest of the surface that's supposed to be the floor is jammed up with all the stuff that used to be in the room. I step forward and stand on an upturned living room chair.

"Why are you wet?" Mama asks me from the kitchen where she's trying to balance the fridge and a wall cabinet before they fall over.

"Went for a run. Why is everything dark?"

"The electricity went," she says. "Thunderstorm."

I crawl the passage to my room and find dry clothing. Three layers of it.

I head northwest, where Daddy said we'd be safe to sleep. It's impossible to walk upright with a house in this position / everything gathers in the corners / we live in a V.

I find the linen closet for a blanket and pillow, then a relatively empty area in the northwest passageway, and I balance myself against the exterior wall of a box and the slanted pieces of corridor under my feet. Once I recline, lying at the angle my jav lands when it sticks into the dirt, I turn on my side, and I close my eyes.

FAMILY WRESTLING

I wake up in NØTIME / it's still pitch-dark / Mama is propped next to me on the slanted, windowless wall. Richard has made a bed out of a pile of old towels—down in the valley of the now-floor. He is singing a song in Portuguese.

"Richard," I whisper.

He sings louder.

"I love you," I say.

"I love you, too," he sings.

"I love all of you," Mama says, her breath aimed right at my nose.

Daddy makes his Somewhere-Else sound. It's hard to know what it means. He uses it for all of Plutchik's emotions.

"We're all pretending to sleep," I say.

"Wishful napping," Mama says. "Your sister used to call it that."

Tiny bombs in the sheltered walls explode at the sound of this word / sister / none of us even flinch.

"She told me that you used to take her into your room at night and stab her with quilting pins," Richard says.

Mama says, "I don't even own quilting pins."

"Me too," I say. "She said when you did it, you'd tell her the whole time that she was ugly."

"Did you ever see me make a quilt?" Mama says.

"She said that you could kill us," I add. "Like really kill us."

Mama says, "I don't even kill spiders."

Richard says, "I was the one who put a scratch in the coffee table. I was ten and was playing with my Matchbox cars. I'm also the one who broke the toilet when I was in seventh grade. It was an accident. I didn't know not to put polymer beads in the drains."

"Such old things to talk about," Daddy says.

"She said you would kill us," I say.

Mama says, "I don't even own a quilt!"

Richard tells the story about being twelve and how sister locked him in the garden shed and how he missed dinner and how mad

Mama was when he finally squeezed his way out the window and
ran in the back door.

"Oh!" Mama says. "I remember that day! I scolded you so
much! I'm sorry, son."

The plywood creaks.

"You told me that you'd been playing baseball," Mama adds.

"When did Richard ever play baseball?" I asked. "I was eight
and I knew he was lying."

X

The only way to get my work done—stop time while everyone is
sleeping / pretend-sleeping—slip away. My crowbar is in the valley of box #7. Next to it is my class ring and chunks of cracked
eyeshadow powder / an old ant trap / a sports bra.

Southeast is the only logical option / opposite direction. That's
my room, and next to it, box #9. Locked from the outside / locked
from the inside.

x equals 334 nails, tonight.

KNOCK / "LATE"

At whatever-o'clock, Richard and Daddy move toward the rest of
the house, still balancing on forty-five-degree-angled walls / floors.
Mama and I are slowly trying to clear up our sleeping mess of pillows, blankets, and hallway flotsam, when I hear a knock on the door.

I walk to the front of the house / look through the window. It's
Carrie. "Do you even turn on your phone or are you just ignoring
me?" she says through the glass. I give her the gimme-a-minute
finger / find my phone in my backpack.

x equals three texts from Carrie:

Where were you at practice?

You okay?

Len says you're not in class. Did you go in this morning or need a ride?

"We're late," she says through the door glass. "Power outage. My alarm failed."

I open the door. The look on her face as she sees me balancing on two slanted walls—inside the diamond of our house with all the foyer furniture and stuff under me—changes from annoyed to pitying.

I look to Daddy, who is standing in the diagonal, upside-down doorway of the kitchen, groggy and still in his boxer-short underwear and a T-shirt. "I'll need a late note."

He looks around as if he will find normal things like a pen and paper in our sinking boat. I sift through the stuff under me in the foyer. We had a coffee mug full of pens on a little table here once. I find a ballpoint and a random index card.

I say, "Here," and hand it to him.

He hovers the pen over the card's surface for a full thirty seconds and says, "I am very sorry, Truda. I cannot find words to write."

I look into his eyes and they are wet.

When he cries, his shoulders shake. I rub his back. The plywood creaks and I can hear nails bending and popping from their holes.

When the maze turns, the fridge clunks against the nearest wall, and stays at the angle in which Daddy and Carmichael had propped it up.

"Hey!" Richard says from somewhere near the southwest conduit.

Daddy continues to cry, but heads east from the kitchen.

I take the paper and pen and go back to Carrie. The floor / wall is still slanted, but becoming flatter / saner.

She says, "What the fuck is going on in there?"

I look past her to the trees in our neighbors' front lawns. Nothing outside the house is turning. Only us. In a tumble dryer set to eternity / insect in our brains / normalized fight / flight. And I became a javelin so I could fly.

I squeeze through to my room and dig through piles of furniture, clothing, papers, and shards of shattered light bulb / nick my index finger / and find something not slept-in to wear.

I stop and write Daddy's note.

Truda Becker was late today because it's still June 23, 2020, and there is no such thing as late. Even when the lights go out. Even if a world record is set. Even if cars still run and supermarkets still sell magazines. Also, never flush polymer beads down the toilet.

I forge his signature at the bottom.

TROJAN HORSE

Len says we should handle Nigel's destruction like a Trojan horse.

"I'm late," Carrie says. "What's the horse?"

Len says, "It's one thing to post this on social media or whatever, but I don't care what some dude-bro in South Dakota thinks of Nigel."

"What's the horse, though?" I ask.

"We invite Nigel in to see the fruits of our labor. Call it a presentation or something. Invite the principal. Once a few of us talk about what we learned in our projects, it's my turn. I run the documentary, and Nigel will be right there, front-row seat."

"And you're Odysseus, rushing out of the horse?"

"Something like that," Len says.

"I like it," Eric says. "But I can't tell how much trouble we're going to get into for it."

"Yeah," Ellie says. "I think we should send it to the board, the administration, and my dad all at the same time. Believe me, that'll work."

The classroom phone beeps twice. We ignore it.

"I'm with Ellie on this. No offense to your horse," I say.

"It's cool. I was just trying to make it an event, you know? But low-key is fine, too."

We get back to Solution Time / were supposed to do Sadness today, and I wasn't looking forward to it / look at me. But since I was late, Eric took the class.

The whiteboard is filled with Sadness feelings in Eric's handwriting. Unmotivated, tired, crying, pessimistic, scared of worse sadness, suicidal, feel like a burden, quiet, reserved, just want to stay in bed, regretful, grief feelings even if no one died, grief feelings if someone has died, wanting to punch things (anger?), rejected, not belonging with other people (no one wants to be with sad people—Eric), end of the world feelings, nothing will ever be right, scream into a pillow, being bitchy, saying depressing things, not saying anything, feels illegal, feels wrong (when my cat died, my grandmother told me it was just a cat—Len), outcast, adults get afraid, adults say we have it better, adults are untrustworthy around teen sadness.

I tell him I appreciate it.

"No, no. You don't get it," Eric says. "If it weren't for your Plutchik's Clock, I wouldn't have figured out the real conclusion for my paper. In one generation, if we do it right, we can change the entire world's general mental health," he says. "This is the solution to fourteen generations of bullshit that we don't have to pass down to our kids. That's our job. Generation fifteen. We'll be the generation who heals."

Healing / not on any syllabus / should be.

The classroom phone beeps again and the secretary says, "Truda Becker, report to the office."

"I wish they'd fuck off. I'm sorry, Eric," I say.

Eric says, "Tru, you broke a world record. Of course you have things to do."

Door opens. A slightly ruffled Nigel tumbles in as if he'd intended to, though we know he was pushed into the room by the athletic director.

"Truda, you're needed in the office," Nigel says. "The mayor's here."

PHOTO OP

I ask Carrie to come with me. The athletic director looks her up and down. She says, "Long jump and triple jump. Carrie. Nice to meet you." He shakes her hand because her outstretched arm / truce / is there.

He walks ahead and Carrie asks, "Why won't you tell me where you went yesterday instead of practice? And what's going on at your house? I don't understand your dad's art."

"Long story about the house. And I quit track. That's why I wasn't there yesterday."

"Quit?"

"Yeah."

"Why?"

"Look at me," I say.

It goes right over her head.

Before she can answer, the athletic director slows down and falls in step with us and asks, "About that world record. Did you know you could do that? Turner says you knew."

"I knew."

"So why didn't you throw that far before?"

"I didn't want to make anyone feel bad," I say.

Waiting for me in the school lobby are the mayor, our state senator, Daddy, and Mama. Daddy is in his Trojan windbreaker / Mama is wearing her psychic outfit, complete with bells at the hem of her skirt. Behind them all, outside in the hedgerow of nondescript evergreen bushes, is Richard, who drove them here. None of them show signs of living in a barn-style hamster wheel / sobbing about it earlier this morning.

I whisper to Mama, "Why is Richard in the bushes?"

"He doesn't want his picture taken, but he wanted to watch. You know how he is."

"It's very nice to meet you!" the mayor says, and shakes my hand. The senator does the same. We get our photos taken in front of the Trojan logo in the hallway in front of the main office. I don't hear a word they say to me.

The whole time, I quit track in my head / fail all my tests in school / decide to stay in bed forever, wherever my bed is, now, in the plywood rotisserie of our house. I have had my AFT3RMATH / I have had my EV3NT / My OR1G1N is coming / be reborn without residue / become who I was meant to be.

Part Three

OR1G1N

Anomalies

THE DISAPPOINTMENT

N3WCLOCK had become so stunningly normal by the day I beat the world record in women's javelin, people hadn't stopped to think about anything new. Schedules didn't change. People didn't change. No one used the fold in time and space as an opportunity for growth mindset / for learning new recipes / taking naps / visiting anywhere they hadn't been before. No solutions were coming out of any classroom other than to hide the problem / make new time just like the old time.

N3WCLOCK is a prosthetic limb / we're pretending it isn't. Looking at a wolf / calling it Grandma.

We just kept working, like ants.

N3WCLOCK workplace timeclocks were made / special chip connects / your sweat lives in Wi-Fi now. Stamp your card / collect your pay / take up a hobby on the weekend. Billions of people believing in something they don't understand / happy with that.

And people call *me* an anomaly.

REST

To understand anything is to understand energy. Solution Time is energy lost / busywork for children. Not for long.

I have discovered Bertrand Russell, thanks to two quotes that Len showed me:

"To realize the unimportance of time is the gate to wisdom."
    —Bertrand Russell

"Immense harm is caused by the belief that work is virtuous."
—Bertrand Russell

—▭—

Russell was a twentieth-century philosopher who wants me to rest / wants us all to rest / wants us all to stop balancing something as ridiculous as workweeks and leisure time / wants us to get bored enough to be creative / learn about ourselves. Wait /

Wait.

If there was a way to change the people in the world, it would have happened by now. It's been nine months since time stopped. Whoever started this thing will to have to shut it down / call it a fail / concede to the fact that we are all too dull to invent anything new—too dull to do something good for ourselves.

The need for Nigel and Solution Time would be gone by the time "The Anomalies" aired on Sunday. I am the anomaly / never dull / who will make this happen.

NO ONE ASKS

It's surprising, but not even Coach Aimee asks me where I was yesterday. We just stretch like normal and run our slow laps and no one is treating me like I'm anything special / just how I like it.

Until Kelly says, "Your interview was cool. What you said about Giselle was really nice. My little brother thinks you're cute and wants to be your boyfriend."

"How old is he?"

"Seven."

I laugh and she laughs and this all feels like a horror movie setup.

"I'm glad they didn't cut that part out," I say. "I didn't see it."

"The part about the special they're doing—about how you're, like, magic? My whole family is going to watch. Did you see the blind girl in Florida who can see now?"

I am being compared to Jesus miracles on American television / Daddy will hammer more nails / Mama will use me for advertising.

Giselle and I walk to the locker room together. Carrie isn't avoiding me / I'm avoiding her / still quitting track.

"You looked great on TV," she says.

"Thanks." I think about telling her that I didn't want to be on TV but that's too hard for most people to understand / I just want to rest / be tucked in by Bertrand Russell.

"I don't know what you are, but I don't think you're a freak," she says. "I think it's rude the way they talked about you. My dad's saying you might be an alien and he's not that dumb, you know? He's just—I don't know."

"He's jealous. And I get it. And I'm glad you don't think I'm an alien. Look. Are my eyelids blinking vertically or horizontally today?"

"Like regular eyes," she says.

"I was kidding."

"It was nice what you said about me," she says.

"I'm going to quit track," I say.

"What? Why?"

I shrug.

I stop by my gym locker and pick up my stuff, go up the steps so I can leave via the front doors / take a lazy walk. Carrie won't see me / drive me home / won't understand Bertrand Russell. The way people are now, the only way they'd consider practicing idleness, timelessness, and creativity is if we tooled the name / B3RTRAND RUSS3LL / invented an app.

JENNIFER

"Why can't they let me have this one thing?" I ask this to a squirrel. I ask a tree / the grass / a blob of dog shit. "Just this one time?"

Instead, I'm a joke / water-cooler conversation / debated / debatable / debased / a teenage girl who did something great / let's interview her dad.

I try to enjoy my walk. The trees are sprouting leaves. The sun is warm.

My phone ringtone thumps with electronic bass and the number has an area code I don't recognize.

"Hello?"

A little girl's voice is on the other end. "Is this Truda Becker?"

"Who's this?"

"My name is Jennifer," she says. "I'm calling from Omaha, Nebraska."

"Okay," I say.

"I'm—uh—I'm the girl who can fly," she says. "Ashley gave me your number because—"

"Because she's trying to get me on the show," I say.

"No," Jennifer says. "Because sometimes I think about flying right into a wall. Or traffic. Or just—I don't know. I'm sad and no one understands."

"Why are you sad?"

"Because I'm a freak?"

"You're not a freak," I say. "You're amazing."

Jennifer is quiet for a while. I can't tell if she's crying / flying into a wall.

"You okay?" I ask.

"Do you think this will ever go away? Like, when time starts again or whatever?"

"I don't know," I say.

She starts to cry. I can hear how ten she is. Little sobs / big tears. I watch a squirrel jump from one tree to another, barely making it to the branch.

"It's going to be okay," I tell her. "Stop thinking about what's going to happen. Just keep flying. It's fun, right?"

"Yeah."

"Then keep doing it."

She sniffles for a while and takes a few controlled breaths. "It's incredible," she says. "Isn't it incredible to be able to do something like this?"

"I just throw a javelin. Flying seems a lot more cool."

"Yeah," she says. "I guess it is."

I'm getting closer to home. I like Jennifer / always wanted a little sister / can't stop being upset about Carrie / wish I was ten again / remember ten and almost cry, myself.

"I have to go now, but you can call me or text if you need to, okay?"

"Okay. Thanks for talking to me."

"Thanks for calling. It's so nice to meet you."

"Keep throwing!" she says.

"Keep flying," I say / we hang up.

BERTRAND RUSSELL'S DINNER MENU

Daddy's blackened Cajun chicken alfredo is not concerned with getting to work on time / golfing on the weekend. The cheese sauce is not judging Daddy for not having a job / for using his time to build boxes to protect his family / making art / even if the art is ugly.

He's not bored / the alfredo is honest as yogurt / that's what happens / B3RTRAND RUSS3LL.

Carmichael is here and in the kitchen / plywood still under us so we don't stomp through the west wall / now floor. Behind him there is a working upright sink that empties into a bucket and one wall cabinet that's temporarily secured to the wall / ceiling at a slight angle / no door. No one has had time to clean, so the linoleum floor / now wall / is filthy, especially in the spots that used to live under appliances and cabinets. The whole house smells vaguely of natural gas.

Carmichael, Daddy, and Richard cleaned out the house as much as they could today. The backyard is now a graveyard of furniture and household things that cannot survive twisted at a 90- / 180- / 270-degree angle.

As we gather for dinner, we all act as if we're having a typical dinner, not in the living room where the carpet is on the wall. Even Carmichael has gotten used to it / is pouring wine into glasses that are balanced on the edge of the fridge door / no normal surfaces left.

"You were not here to set table," Daddy says to me.

"Sorry I was late. I walked home slowly," I say.

"Are you okay?" Mama asks. "You must be exhausted."

"They're doing a special on Sunday night," Richard says. "Maybe 60 Minutes will call you!"

There is no rest / now I know who wrote to Ashley, anyway.

"Do you still have clients this week?" I ask Mama.

"I have three tomorrow afternoon," she says. "A cat, a grand-mother, and a life-coaching session."

"What do cats tell you from the afterlife?" Richard asks.

Carmichael says, "Meow!" and Daddy and Mama laugh and I think it's wrong for Mama to take money from people and lie about their dead cats and grandmothers.

"They actually say more than that," she says. "They send love to their owners. And gratitude." She takes a bite of bread. "You'd be surprised what animals can tell us." She looks sad / I wonder where Beano is / if the trade was worth it for her.

We eat in quiet and I chew my Cajun chicken slowly.

"I love you and am grateful for you," I say to Mama / am in-spired by dead cats. She reaches her hand to my face and strokes my cheek with the back of her index finger.

We smile at each other.

To understand anything is to understand energy / smiles are conduit / frowns are conduit / compliments can power a toaster / water heater / whole town.

"You are both so beautiful," Daddy says, "I could cry." Daddy can only pretend / hammer nails / give compliments. Nine months ago, Mama left / he quit his job / time stopped. Now Mama is back / what comes next we don't know.

"Are you staying now?" Richard asks Mama.

"I am."

"Why did you leave?" he asks.

"We will answer this at meeting," Daddy says.

Richard's frown is conduit / too many family meetings.

"I am honored by your invitation," Carmichael says.

Mama's frown is conduit / to understand anything is to understand energy / is to understand jealousy.

"If you didn't have to go to work or college, would you be bored?" I ask.

All four of them look at me, wondering who I was asking / why I'm changing the subject. I make the I'm-asking-all-of-you gesture and wait.

"I'd probably watch too much TV," Mama says. "If we still had a TV."

"I'd sleep more. And probably play video games," Richard says. "I miss video games."

Carmichael and Daddy think.

I say to Richard, "You'd learn more Portuguese."

"True."

I look at Mama. "You'd probably learn something new about tarot cards or palmistry or something."

"I've been wanting to take another course for years," she says. "Or take up oil painting."

"I do not get bored," Carmichael says. "I keep busy, always."

Daddy nods. That's his answer, too. Clearly / look around / plywood carnival fun house / not moving forward.

Someone has made my bed and tidied my room. My guess would be Mama because she put things in places only a mother could choose. She even put my bathroom bucket in a place that offers privacy. Tonight's family meeting—we will get an answer / I already know the answer. To understand anything is to understand energy.

I lie on my bed and daydream about Bertrand Russell. Earth falling into a fold in time and space suited Daddy just fine / still does. It would suit me fine, too, if I didn't have to go to school. I could use some boredom / time to throw things really far / wish I could fly like Jennifer—I'd never stop.

The intercom squeaks from the wall / floor under my bed now. It's meeting time.

THREE-QUARTERS THERE

We're in the living room. Carmichael sits on the couch with Daddy now that Mama has her chair back. All other furniture is gone except the old kitchen table / pushed to the edge so we have more room.

Richard is already here / yelling. I wish I could push him into the AFT3RMATH, but everyone needs to find it in their own way.

"You can't just be a yo-yo like this! Moving in and out. Think of what Tru needs for once, you know?"

"Hi," I say.

"She's leaving again," Richard says.

"I am not leaving again," Mama says. "I didn't even say that. I asked to see your phone."

Carmichael says, "I would like to see your phone, Richard."

Richard says no.

Daddy reaches into Richard's hands and takes the phone. Richard jumps on him. There is wrestling / Carmichael joins in. I look at Mama. We both remember the day of the bird / the day Richard cried all the way through dinner—even with extra tapioca pudding.

I don't even sit down / this isn't a family meeting / I already know why she left.

It wasn't just the bird. It was never just the bird. We are the birds.

Daddy was usually immune to sister's screwdriver / her rages / her lies. During the kiosk job, she turned on Mama. Mama talks to dead cats / grandmothers / was not equipped to handle that sort of thing.

Sometimes things are that simple / a switched person can be flipped / on / off.

I look at Carmichael, who is back on the couch now. Richard has gone to box #11. Daddy has Richard's phone / is reading texts from sister. I ask, "So, why is our house turning?"

Carmichael answers, "Lies."

"Whose lies?"

"I cannot tell," he says. "There are so many."

—▭—

When I check my phone, Carrie has sent me links to two websites. Both are about "The Anomalies." I swear if I ever hear that word again, I'll spontaneously combust. Ten bucks says 60 Minutes will not be interested in that.

Listen. We're all anomalies.

Look at Daddy / Mama / Richard. None of us are really who we say we are.

Mama is no psychic. Daddy is no builder. Richard is no scholar. And I am no national teenage hero. We're just a family / pocked with shrapnel / our bathrooms are in the backyard now. Even Carmichael isn't a plumber / he's got a CPA certificate on the wall of his living room / hates numbers.

The anomalies are every one of us. Every day. None of this is normal. Nothing is normal. No one can define normal / anomalies are impossible with no control group.

NAILS

I don't know if Carmichael and Daddy are teaming up, but there's more plywood / more boxes than one man could construct in a day / we live in a giant four-ply kiosk that doesn't sell anything but confusion. The only way to get anywhere is to stop time and pull nails for extra hours.

I get 659 out before I can't lift the crowbar anymore.

We Are Psych Team

THE EMAIL

All of us agreed that we couldn't just send a random video to the school board. We had to claim it.

Len says, "Like the way terrorists claim—uh—"

Eric says, "Probably not a good comparison."

"We should write a letter," Ellie says. "Short and sweet." She opens her laptop.

Carrie says, "To Whom It May Concern."

Ellie says, "We have attached a video to this—"

"It's a short film, not a vine," Len says.

Ellie says, "We have attached a short documentary film to this email."

"Too big to attach," Len says. "We'll link it."

Ellie deletes. Starts again. "We are Psych Team—five students who have been using our Solution Time to study how the human mind could solve the time problem."

Eric jumps in. "Sadly, due to the advisor, Nigel Andrews, we can no longer continue with our projects or our study of how time affects the human mind. He has acted—uh—"

"He has been a bully every day he's come to class and mocks our projects and our personal selves, leaving us deflated and depressed," Carrie says. "He recently told not only our class, but *all* classes of Trojans, that he plans to fail us and hurt our futures by doing so."

"That might need to go shorter," Len says.

Carrie says, "Cut the part about failing us."

I say, "Let's end it. How about Mr. *Andrews has no business being around children?*"

"Add this as a PS," Len says. "If you don't act on this, we will move on to phase two. After seeing this, we do not think you want to see phase two."

Ellie screen mirrors it to the whiteboard. We read it. We cut it up / streamline it.

Len says, "Can I cut it back even further?" and Ellie hands him her laptop / he edits.

"When do we send it?" I ask.

"Now," Len says. "Right now."

> We are Psych Team.
> Please watch this documentary.
> Nigel Andrews must go.
> You do not want to see phase two.

FREAK SCHOOL

Len walks with me to my locker. "So, I saw the trailer for the 60 *Minutes* special they're doing on anomalies," he says. "They were asking around for footage of your throw."

"No one has footage," I say.

"I have footage," he says.

"You didn't send it to them, did you?"

He shakes his head.

"Send it to me," I say.

"On it," he says, and moves toward his next class / head down / pressing the send button.

I have English and I don't feel like going to class. Something about the possibility of seeing myself throw makes me edgy / nervous / panicked. My phone vibrates when I'm ten steps from the classroom door / bell about to ring / don't even know the title of the story I was supposed to read last night / stuck in a never-ending rotisserie family meeting.

My English teacher is at the door, greeting students like he always does / fist bumps and high fives. He sees me / I see him / I can't go in.

Freeze! Nobody move.

As I walk through the hallway of motionless high school students, I see they are all anomalies, too. Tasha Kirsch is an anomaly of friendship / is friends with *everyone* / even me. Kevin is frozen mid-flex / an anomaly of self-adoration of his biceps. That tall kid who sings in the choir / his range is impossible from falsetto to baritone / an anomalous pharynx. Heather Flake is totally vaping weed tucked into the entrance to the girls bathroom / straight-A student / runs most clubs / is completely baked / anomalous stoner. Abnormal is what high schoolers do, no matter how normal we may seem / it's our job.

The minute they put us in this building we're expected to be something we aren't. Interested / engaged / athletic / baby grown-ups with the will to be social and succeed in life. The building acts factory / as if it can turn out capable adults, and it will. Adults like Richard / our rifle / normal on the outside / interiorly, needs an exterminator. Adults like our sister / an assortment of bombs / an anomaly to the truth. Adults like Mama and Daddy / broken and shamed for nothing but being human / having never been given human skills / Plutchik's Clock. This building is a swimming class that only teaches its students how to float on their backs / keep heads above water / no bayonets / unprepared for a full-frontal attack / life / but I know how to multiply fractions.

I find an empty classroom and sit at the desk closest to the door and play Len's footage of my throw. It's a minute long. I watch it ten times / ten minutes / my form isn't that bad / I just look determined. I close in on the jav as it flies / look for myself / I am there, next to the jav / flying. I am also still on the field next to Coach Aimee and Giselle, watching it fly.

The only thing anomalous about this throw / ability / determination is the fact that I don't want to be like anyone else / want to throw like anyone else / want to walk like anyone else / you get the picture. The only thing anomalous about me / Truda Becker / is that it took me too long to show anyone what I was made of / now they think I'm made of magic.

I start time again and go to English class / my only option / can't hide all day / fist-bump on my way through the door.

The story we were supposed to read was about a kid who was determined to hurt his parents by failing, but only hurt himself / propaganda / propaganda / always a moral to a story that no one is actually living.

GROWTH MINDSET II

I don't even like being on the track team / quit seven hundred times today in my head.

We stretch in the gym / the gym is propaganda / banners and trophies from things that don't matter / energy confined by painted lines.

"Meet on Tuesday," Coach Aimee says. "Who's ready to beat their own numbers?"

When everyone yells "I AM!" I mouth the words / quit track team again.

We move outside for some running and sprinting and my spikes feel heavy.

Carrie walks with me. "I had that feeling again today," she says, "like time slowed down or something. My fingers tingled. I asked Henry if he felt it, too. He sits next to me. He said he felt like throwing up all of a sudden."

"Bummer. I hope you didn't catch anything from him," I say.

"So you don't feel it at all?"

"No. When was it?"

"At the beginning of first period," she says.

"Right after we sent the letter?"

"Yeah."

I say, "That letter had me jumpy all day."

"Ellie thinks we'll get in trouble," she says.

"We might."

"You don't seem to care," she says.

"I live in a plywood tilt-a-whirl, Carrie."

"Yeah. I guess that's hard," she says. "I mean—to care about anything else."

"I care, but I don't care about Nigel. He gets what he earned, you know? Just like the rest of us."

I did / didn't mean for that to come out so curtly / *Look at me.* Carrie notices something is wrong / I start running laps.

My eye contact / nothing but the jav. I stare at it even when Coach Aimee is talking about new throwing order. I think she says the new throwing order is that I go last.

So I go last.

My form still resembles a choking water fowl. I throw it clear into the woods. Probably about three hundred and twenty feet. Coach Turner is a proud-grandfather type / Aimee plays the part of a jealous sibling.

"Hot damn!" he says.

"Go get it," Aimee says, and points to the woods beyond the shot-put area.

I walk into the woods and it's not like I imagined / a lot of trash on the ground / remnants of small parties. There is a pair of panties / an empty six-pack / a soggy hamburger roll.

As I walk back onto the field and around the outside of the track toward the throwing area, I see Giselle, Kelly, and Petra spike-throwing and shoulder-rolling / tumbleweed of angry girls with ponytails. I keep my eye on the jav / it is no longer me.

x equals how I was the jav so I could fly.

x equals how I can fly by myself.

TEENAGE CHILL SPOT

"Don't disappear today," Carrie says to me. "We're going to Mc-Donald's."

I almost say no, but remember that I don't want to go home. Nothing wrong with home—Mama and Daddy and Richard will be there. Maybe Carmichael. I love all those people. But the boxes / I am done with splinters / family meetings.

I text that I won't be home until ten and then promise not to look for a reply / look at my callused hands and think about how many nails I've pulled / how much time I've spent disassembling Daddy's project / whatever it is.

WHAT YOU DON'T KNOW ABOUT THE BOXES
Daddy knew he was losing a battle /
was unprepared for the ambush.
The boxes are frenzy.
The boxes are safety.
The boxes are structure.
The boxes are magic / erase memory
the way Mama talks to dead cats—
the boxes are a scam /
fake love affairs.
Nothing will be right
until the boxes are gone.

Because it's Friday night, McDonald's is packed with other teenagers from our school and the neighboring school district. Carrie and I wait in line and the tall kid from school—the choirboy with the anomalous pharynx—works there and smiles at me / reminds me that every person in the place might recognize me.

And so they should. Today I threw a javelin into the woods and broke my own world record. Usually I want to disappear /

instead / I look him right in the eye and smile. He smiles back. The feeling I have after this exchange is something I am not used to / confidence.

I grew it myself.

Carrie and I keep exchanging looks because it's too loud to talk. There must be fifty loud teenagers in the space in front of the counter. She hands me her phone, where she's typed *I'm sorry about what I said Wednesday at lunch.* I nod and check my options.

    I.   Carrie could be lying to me.
    II. Carrie could be telling the truth.
    III. It doesn't really matter.

She types more into the phone. *That tall guy just gave you the love eyes.*

I grab the phone / write back *Stop trying to get me to like people just because they smile at me.* We wait and wait and finally land in front of the giant choirboy / order / pay / receive / find a table near the back door. I see people looking at me / stand up straighter / push my shoulders back / refuse to be ashamed of being Truda Becker anymore.

The insect is still there / is simply too tiny to matter.

I'd planned on having a conversation with Carrie in her kitchen when she invited me out. I didn't know she'd planned to eat here / no place for a conversation.

But she tries.

"So is your dad's art project, like, also a carnival ride or something?"

I can't answer her because I've just taken a huge bite of my Big Mac.

"Because the other day, it didn't look like it was working right," she says. "I mean, if it's a ride or something supposed to be fun. You looked terrified."

"Let's talk about it at your house," I say.

"We can't go to my house," she says. "My parents are there."

"We can't just go to your room?" We always just go to her room.

"They told me not to come home until ten."

"Oh."

"I can't tell if that's normal or not," she says.

I shrug. I almost suggest we go to my house / forget we don't have bathrooms anymore.

We eat and listen to the conversations around us. No one is staring or noticing me the way I feared they would / it's okay to be good at something / set a world record / eat a Big Mac. Carrie looks at her phone.

She says, "Len and Eric want to meet up somewhere." She checks her school email. "Still no reply from the school board."

—▭—

The stadium is quiet at night / no party in the woods / no arguing field judges. The moon is rising and it's getting dark slowly—stars pop out one by one.

"I think they should have answered by now," Len says.

"I don't," Eric says. "It'll probably make my mom cry. She cries enough."

"My dad will take care of it," Ellie says.

"They're being quiet to scare us," I say.

"Doesn't scare me," Len says.

"Nothing scares you," Carrie says.

"Do you think we should enter phase two before Monday?" Len asks.

"I think we should wait," I say.

"Why?" Eric asks.

"Because by Monday, everything could be different," I say.

Eric pulls out his ukulele and strums some chords and Len and Ellie talk for a while and Carrie sings a little to Eric's song and I stand up and stretch my arms to get rid of the tension / ready me for the nails I'll pull tonight.

We chill out for an hour or so / debate phase two. For twenty minutes, they're all for phase two / shaming Nigel in the town square / internet. The following twenty minutes they lean toward waiting until Monday. Every time they ask me what I think / I think we should wait. To understand anything is to understand energy. Every time I say "I think we should wait," there is energy.

Twenty minutes later / Len dares me to throw a javelin / hands one right to me.

We walk down to the field / Len pulls out his camera / I say *no cameras.*

I start my run from as far back as I can / bounce / three steps / throw. My friends / hands over their eyes / squinting / no halogens / searching the darkness. It is gone / the jav is gone / beyond the woods / beyond the highway on the other side / beyond the Target department store and the place where Daddy buys meat / beyond the residue / beyond state lines / beyond the oceans / beyond this plane / my mother could talk to it now, if she wants.

Psych Team takes a final vote.

We will wait until Monday.

SOLUTION

Daddy and Mama are on the front lawn when Carrie drops me off at ten. They're sitting on lawn chairs as if they're enjoying a sunny day in Miami. It's only forty-five degrees out here and I'm positive that the house has finally collapsed on itself and I will have to sleep outside for the night / the car is gone / wonder where Richard is.

"We are watching for meteors," Daddy says.

I look around. "The backyard would work a lot better. Can't see anything with these streetlights."

"We like it here," Mama says.

They are holding hands between chairs, and Daddy is drinking a glass of red wine.

"We are finding solution," Daddy says.

I enter through the me-shaped hole. Our house is still carpet-on-the-west-wall / 270 degrees turned. With Daddy outside / holding hands / Richard out for a drive / it's the perfect time.

SPLINTERS

I pull nail after nail after nail. Psych Team will wait until Monday / I will not. Daddy's boxes must go / today / tomorrow / before I have to shit into a bucket again.

I hear Richard arrive home and soon after, I hear Mama and Daddy come inside and the three of them talking in the kitchen. I work near box #9 / her room / her not-room / attempt to collapse it from underneath / seems dumb / willing splinters / reward for destroying the remote controller.

Splinters / are / reward.

Box #9 is a power station / nuclear / the energy has a half-life of forever.

It's just memories / memories are the insect / just one sting can kill you / depends on the bug. My flying / jav / Paleolithic removed the bug. I'm not sure what to do with the rest of my family / will have to find their own bugs on their own time. This is how I will save them / I will open box #9 and let the energy out.

Daddy will cry / the house will turn / Mama will stop being a mothering yo-yo.

Richard will find a way to remove the screwdriver from his back.

When they're all in bed, I take a break / kitchen / ham-and-cheese sandwich and Daddy's home-fried potato chips. I stretch my arms and neck and back / drink milk out of the carton.

An hour later, the noise is impossible / interior of box #9 collapses / Mama always said she wanted a guest room. I freeze time / just to stand here and be satisfied.

While time is frozen, I move my way through the hallway to my room / pulling nails. Box #8 is already done / the bathroom. I take a left toward the silent living room / box #2 / no air in the vents and no wind outside / the world is frozen. I start in the corner and stand on the kitchen table to reach the high nails.

I hear a noise behind me / turn around.

Daddy is in the kitchen, cutting a piece of crumb cake / has his toolbelt on / not sleepwalking / can't see me. I freeze / like everyone else in the world right now / thanks to me / this is weird.

Cleanup

DADDY'S BREAKFAST SOFTWARE

Carmichael arrives at sunrise. Daddy makes him breakfast / alarm clock for the rest of us / smells so good, we arrive with our hands out.

"Carmichael asked for breakfast burritos!" Daddy says.

We sit around the kitchen table, still in the living room on plywood so it doesn't fall through the floor / wall. We eat small, delicious, homemade tortillas filled with God. I stare at the corner where I stood only hours ago while time was stopped, watching Daddy carve a midnight snack. I look from the corner to the kitchen.

Daddy explains that it's cleanup day. "Sunny day with nice warm to clean our things," he says.

"I'm starting with Tru in her room," Mama says.

"I will work with Richard," Daddy says.

Carmichael smiles. I look from the corner to the kitchen. Then Daddy.

Corner / kitchen / Daddy.

x equals *Freeze!* NOBODY MOVE.

He's mid-sentence when everyone freezes. He only notices I did it at all when I start time again / nearly instantly / looks like a glitch in his software.

But he knows / and I know / we try to avoid eye contact but end up staring at each other. He must know about all the other times I did it / didn't say a thing. Daddy / an anomaly like me / can stop time / I don't understand this and I don't want to.

INSIDE OUT

"We can't even keep the bed?" I ask Mama.

"Not for now. Not inside."

I sit on it and even though my window is sideways / my sockets are in the floor and ceiling / "Ooo!" / emptying my room feels like I'm moving out before it's time.

We put my clothing into black bags. Mama puts them in her car for organizational purposes, she says, but every cell in my body thinks she will kidnap my clothing / replace it with skirts with bells on the edge. I ask myself what Robert Plutchik would do.

"Can we talk?" I ask.

Mama is standing, and I motion for her to sit.

"I don't trust you," I say. "I want to trust you but I don't."

"I'm not going to leave again," she says. "My shaman told me to stay and heal the family."

"Can you really do that kind of thing?"

"Yes."

Look at her / more serious than ever.

"But you still don't trust me," she says. "Which is smart. I walked out of here at the worst time. For you. For your father. For your brother. I was selfish, I guess, but I would have never survived had I stayed."

She looks even more serious now. I don't know what to say. Everything I ever thought about her is mixed up with everything I ever heard about her / I heard a lot.

"You want to heal but you're not sure if it's time," she says. "If you heal too soon, the bad energy could come and fuck it all up again, right? But if you wait, you could lose your chance at being happy in the here and now of your life."

I nod a little / none of this is rocket science.

She smiles. "Let's empty this dresser and get Carmichael to move the furniture out." We shove the clothes and the weird contents of my top two drawers / mostly ponytail holders and old makeup / notes from school, into two bags. I find an envelope / letter from my sister. I move to put it into the trash pile.

"I know what that is," Mama says.

Purple envelope / everyone would know.

"Yes, it's purple so I know who it's from. But I know what it says," she says. "Or I know what it did." She fiddles with a burr on her fingernail. "It made you scared."

Again, not a mystery.

"Do you know why the house is turning?" I ask.

"I do." She nods and we close up the two black bags. Carmichael and Richard arrive and move furniture out. Mama and I keep ourselves busy.

"Is it me? Am I making the house turn?"

"Not at all," she says / stops and studies me. "You're much too busy trying to fix things with that crowbar at night."

"So what's doing it, then?"

"The house is turning because it knows we're coming for it."

I want to tell her more, but something stops me.

"You still don't trust me," she says. "But you'll have to soon. I can't fix this on my own."

"Tell me what's making the house turn."

"The boxes," she corrects, "are turning because of lies."

"Whose lies?"

"Everyone's. But mostly your father's."

"Daddy is the most honest person I ever met," I say. Fresh yogurt / tortillas / makes his own soap.

"He is, yes. That's true," she says. "But when he built these boxes, he was building a lie. Thought he could keep you all separate from each other to solve the problem. That's not how to solve problems."

"Family meetings don't solve problems, either."

"They do. As long as everyone is open."

"You never told us the reason you left," I say. "Doesn't seem very open to me."

"That's because you know why I left."

Desperate people will say anything. Sister said anything / especially during the kiosk job. She was desperate for destruction / never felt special like Mama. Or Daddy. Richard had his good grades. I was simply younger and cuter. She was born empty. Bad energy. Circuits with shorts. Told a psychic woman so many lies that it blocked all her chakras and made her deaf.

"Why didn't you take me with you?"

"You weren't ready yet. Like Richard isn't ready now and I wasn't ready until you set me straight on Friday."

Daddy comes through on the intercom speaker. "Carmichael has asked more breakfast burritos. These will ready in fifteen minutes. How many for you?"

Mama says, "I'll take two, please."

I say, "I'll have two, too."

"Yes!" he says. "Thank you for order!"

Mama giggles / shakes her head / says, "He deserves so much better than what he got."

DADDY'S BREAKFAST DRIVE-THRU MENU

I don't know what breakfast burritos should taste like in a world where Mama is actually psychic. I suddenly want to put my palms in front of her and ask her to read them while doing my tarot cards and a decent chakra balancing.

"We also have orange juice and pineapple juice! Do not forget to pick up with order!" Daddy says.

Richard is out in the backyard with Carmichael. They are cleaning the bathroom fixtures / we will have the cleanest toilets in town.

"Look at his aura," Mama says to me / pointing to Daddy. "He's so ready."

I look at him / his aura / have no idea what a ready aura looks like. All I can see is him flipping tortillas with his left hand while his right makes more eggs for the filling / maybe that's ready.

EMPTY

Because we started so early, my room is completely empty by an hour after Daddy's second breakfast-burrito cycle. Mama and I work to music she puts on / sounds like something Len would listen to. We move to the bathroom and remove any personal things from the cabinet. She grabs a plastic-wrapped four-pack of toilet paper that didn't get ruined in any of the turning / throws it into her overstuffed station wagon.

We move toward box #9 / when we get there, it's gone. No door / no way in / no way out / no room / no box / no sister.

Mama says, "This is how we should see things now."

"That must be hard for you."

Mama makes a noise like it isn't.

"She's still your daughter," I say.

"She's a very old spirit sent to us. Probably sent to me because they thought I could handle her."

"They?" I ask.

"Don't worry about it. Know this," she says. "She may have been born here, grown here, and done her damage here, but never did you deserve an ounce of it."

We are doubting my mother together, you and I.

"I should have put her in my car and driven as far away as I could back on the day I knew for sure," she says. "Which was probably the bird incident. Your father could have raised you and Richard. I could have at least taken her away so she didn't do so much damage."

I start to cry / something in her voice / she's not lying. "I kinda hate you for not doing that," I say.

"I kinda hate me for not doing that, too," she says. "Your father was never on board. His love for me was so big, he started with the boxes. Said it would solve things. Always with the ideas, your father. Smart as hell, can build anything, has no grasp on the human emotional process."

"He makes excellent lasagna but cannot feel," I say.

FAMILY MEETING LUNCH MENU

Late lunch / pretend-2:00 p.m. / Daddy has made us all kinds of tiny sandwiches. He pours wine for Carmichael, himself, and Mama. Richard and I get water. Richard is filthy except for his hands / has dirt on his forehead / his eyes look clear.

The kitchen table is gone from the living room / we sit on the floor / wall / plywood that keeps us from falling through.

Mama says, "Another family meeting. Not as comfortable

without furniture, but it's good to be in a clean space." Her voice echoes around the emptiness.

"If we have one more family meeting this week, I will lose my shit," Richard says.

"This should be the last one," Mama says.

Carmichael says, "Concordia, I have always respected you. You are honest and remind me of my great-grandmother. She was smart and beautiful. I hope you do not mind me saying."

"She is the most beautiful woman on planet," Daddy says. "You do not need to tell me."

Richard laughs.

Daddy turns to him and asks, "Where do you go in car at night?"

Richard stops laughing.

"I check odometer," Daddy says. "Also, I find long blond hair in car. Truda is brunette."

"Well, shit," Mama says. "Do you finally have a girlfriend?"

Richard stays quiet / looks like he's about to crap his pants. "Why do you look so scared?" I ask. "You're twenty-one and have a girlfriend. There's nothing wrong with that."

Carmichael looks to Daddy. "You said you would talk to him about this, friend."

"I did," Daddy says. "We had man-to-man."

Richard still looks terrified / I am beginning to think this isn't a normal girlfriend.

"Can we see a picture? Can we meet her?" I ask.

"Honey, I know what happened back then made you all fucked up," Mama says. "But you're a normal guy. I promise."

Carmichael says, "What you did is in the past."

"I didn't *do* anything!" Richard says / his me-shaped hole.

"Can someone tell me what's going on?" I say.

"You heard the rumor," Richard said.

"Was it true?"

"No!" Richard says. He makes a frustrated sound and adds, "It's complicated."

"Did you actually like her or something?" I ask.

"I really liked her," he says. "When I thought she was sixteen, yeah. Her texts were so funny."

"Oh," I say / imagine Giselle as funny once / can't grasp it.

Mama says, "Please tell me this new secret girlfriend is over the age of sixteen."

"Jesus!" Richard says. "She's not my girlfriend and, yes, she's over sixteen. Okay? Is that enough?"

"Why is her hair in my car if she is not girlfriend?" Daddy asks.

"Why are you so freaked out about having a girlfriend?" I ask.

"Look at how you all are! It's like an interrogation! But you're telling me it's normal."

"You're the one sneaking out and not acting like this is normal," Mama says.

"You're acting like the rumor was true," I say.

Carmichael points to Richard and then me. "Tell her whole story. No secrets."

My insides twist up.

Richard looks like he's going to yell / cry / act out a Portuguese tragedy. Then his shoulders relax and he takes a deep breath. "Part of it *was* true," he says. "I *did* go to the rec center to pick Giselle up. It *was* six in the morning. Only she wasn't waiting for me *and* she wasn't sixteen. That's when sister showed up."

"Oh," I say. Richard / the rec center / was booby-trapped / Eris.

Richard sighs. "She had screenshots of all the texts we'd sent—she got them from Giselle's phone—and then she told me Giselle was thirteen. She had a list of demands."

"Demands?" I say.

"Like blackmail," Mama says.

"I said no," he says. "I was so upset. I was scared. I was a lot of things, I guess. So she spread the rumor and somehow Giselle's parents found out. I don't even know. I spent most of that time trying to hide from the whole world."

Daddy clears his throat. "I should have not let you hide," he says.

"You wouldn't have been able to stop me," Richard answers.

"But look at how much shame," Daddy says. "You did not do something wrong. Your sister did. This does not explain why you allow her to talk to you."

Mama says, "Or why you're hiding a girlfriend now, three years later."

Richard, our rifle, can't handle all this truth in one place. His Plutchik's Clock is spinning like a Twister spinner.

Mama says, "You don't have to tell us about your girlfriend. But you have to stop listening to your sister. She's controlled your mind for too long."

Richard stands up / shame on his face turned to rage. "She's family," he says. "The only family I have left who isn't crazy. Look at you three! He's building a plywood prison, she's setting world records, and you," he spits at Mama, "are a fraud and a liar."

"In your pocket are four things," Mama says. "A penny, a rock from a walk you took with your girlfriend two weeks ago by a lake, a piece of wrapped chewing gum, and a condom."

Richard goes to say something / puts his hand in the pocket of his jeans.

"Your sister told you so many lies you can't succeed. You don't know who you really are. You had such good energy as a boy. I know it's still there. She covered it with her energy, is all."

"It is my fault," Daddy says / on the verge of tears / bellowing. "Your mother knew what to do many years back. I would not allow it."

Richard looks to me. I look back at him / don't know what to say. "I'm sorry, Tru. You're not crazy. None of you are. I just can't—it feels so mean to just drop her. We went through a lot together."

"You only went through things she caused," I say. "It's a setup."

He looks at Mama and Daddy. "If she's so sick, why didn't you get her help?"

Mama chuckles in a sad way / Daddy, too.

I say, "They did."

"Do you know how many times they investigated your father and me?" Mama says. "Child services, the police"—Daddy shudders at the word—"psychiatrists calling us to tell us we were the problem because we— Ugh. I can't even repeat it."

"These people nearly took you and Truda away from us," Daddy says. "She said we starved her and many worse. Many, many worse."

"So we tried," Mama says. "But psychology didn't work."

Richard says, "Huh. I didn't know that. I guess you should have told us."

I look around me at the plywood. "Even if they'd have told us, she would have found a way to make you believe what she wanted. Come on. How many back-seat car rides have we done together?"

Richard nods / knows / remembers. "I always felt like I had to choose a side and it always had to be hers," he says.

"And your head was so covered in shame," Daddy says, "that you fell in love with a little girl."

Richard, our rifle, puts his head in his hands. If you look hard enough, you can see a million screwdrivers stuck into him / he's been misfiring all this time / sight's set off-kilter. He reaches for his phone and opens it. He goes to his contacts and blocks our sister's number.

"What do you feel?" I ask.

"Scared."

"Why?"

"Because she's going to be so angry."

Mama says, "She was born angry. She'll die angry. She'll be born into some other unsuspecting family angry, and die angry again. It's her destiny. Centuries of bad energy."

"Can't you save her with your powers?" Richard asks / snarky.

"Are you gonna tell us about your girlfriend?" I ask. "I'd really like to meet her."

"Like I can bring her here," he says.

Carmichael laughs like this is the end of a movie / slaps his knee.

Richard tells us: They met on campus / she's twenty-three / she's funny / gets straight-A grades like him. Ten seconds / no name / at least he didn't say it all in Portuguese.

Mama smiles / says, "She sounds lovely."

Daddy makes his Somewhere Else noise in agreement.

Richard says, "I'm sorry about being so stubborn. I was scared. I really thought I might be what everyone said I was."

I notice an anomaly / we are listening to one another.

I notice an anomaly / Mama isn't completely psychic, or if she is, she hasn't mentioned what happened on the couch of the townhouse when I was ten. She looks at me as if she knows what I'm thinking, but she will wait until I tell her. This is only fair / nothing I can do about it now / boundaries / heal / rest.

Mama says, "Today we rebuild." She looks at Daddy / locks eyes / inhales / exhales. "It starts with you, my love. You need to tell us what's troubling you so much that our home has become a carnival ride."

Daddy swats the idea. "I do not believe in this American sharing."

Mama gives him the look of a confident bear.

Daddy starts to laugh, too. He says, "I am very sorry to all of you. Carpet on wall. No toilets." He shakes his head. "I am builder with no work. Father with no family. I talk at food, mostly. I dance with wooden spoon of my mother's. I missed you, Concordia, and am glad you have come home."

"And I'm so sorry I left with no explanation," she says to us.

Mama explains that she and Daddy had a long talk / deliberations after the bird-stabbing. "Most other parents wouldn't catch it," she says. "But I did. And I knew what I had to do." She explains Daddy wouldn't let her / how it got worse with age / how she came to the decision to say *Don't call me.* "I couldn't cope with her while he was off at that mall. She knew it and did everything to break me."

"The kiosks wouldn't let me think!" Daddy says, half a mouthful of tiny sandwich.

"You didn't sleep for a month," Mama says. "You were not yourself at all. I know, sweetheart."

Daddy softens at *sweetheart* and his shoulders drop. "I did not know what to do. A man must know what to do."

At this, he puts his Somewhere-Else head into his Somewhere-Else hands and sobs into Carmichael's lap / Carmichael rubs his friend's head / the house starts creaking / turning / Daddy's tiny sandwiches start to tumble off their plate / wineglasses are quickly gathered by Mama.

FINAL TURN

I have never seen my father cry this way / raised to believe only toddlers and teenage girls did this / never saw it on TV / thought I was a freak for those nights in my room where I just can't stop. I don't look directly at him, but from the sound, I can tell Carmichael's jeans are full of snot and drool and shame.

Mama reaches over and ruffles his hair. Even Richard puts his hand on Daddy's back and rubs in circles.

Box #2 / the living room turns slowly / Richard, Mama, and I rise into squat position / try to balance. Daddy and Carmichael stay on the floor / as it lifts to become the wall again, Carmichael scooches himself toward the corner, coaxing Daddy along with him. Daddy cries and cries / wails like grief / lifts his right hand

and hits the floor for his pain. To understand anything is to understand energy.

Mama stumbles toward the corner and Richard catches her before she falls. She looks at him / holds his face in her hands / says,
"You deserved a better childhood. I'm sorry."

This makes Daddy cry harder / I didn't even think he could
hear us.

By the time Daddy stops crying, the house has righted itself. In
the living room, the carpet is finally back under our feet / we no
longer have to crouch to get through sideways doorways.

To understand energy is to understand yourself / we are all
Paleolithic.

"Emotion causes such hunger!" Daddy says. Richard hands him
the plate of tiny sandwiches. We all sit, carpet beneath us, backs
against the walls—some plywood, some plaster—and recover.
Daddy passes the sandwiches around. Mama puts the wineglasses
in the five-gallon bucket Daddy has been using as a sink in the
kitchen.

I look at the switch—covered in boxes. I look how Daddy built
the rest from there / secured the boxes with each layer / made
it impossible. The only way to get to the switch is to collapse the
whole structure / he is a very smart man.

I walk to box #7 and find my crowbar in the corner of my
turned bedroom / go back to the living room / Daddy still
slumped on Carmichael's shoulder..

"We destroy the boxes today," I say. "All of them."

Richard leaves and reappears with two crowbars and claw hammers from the shed / hands them out.

We begin the search for our precision-built home underneath planks of denial and shame / each of us in a different room. Mama starts in the foyer. I start in my room. Richard starts in his. Carmichael and Daddy do the kitchen first / not much work to be done after the last week / and the living room. Daddy says he will go to the hardware store for supplies at four o'clock.

When N3WCLOCK tells Richard that it's four o'clock, we all meet back in the kitchen. Nothing has collapsed yet / Daddy used too many nails.

My phone rings. It's Carrie.

"Hey, I just got a call from some woman at 60 Minutes. Did you know they're doing a special tomorrow night?"

"Did you talk to her?"

"Not really," Carrie answers. "I just told her that you're amazing."

"You didn't tell her about last night, did you?" I wonder whether the javelin is circling the Earth now / a satellite / not a missile / no target / just flight.

"No. Last night is Psych Team's secret."

"You're not mad at me anymore?" I ask / immediately feel like a needy, brainwashed victim of trickery. But then / to understand anything is to understand energy / good energy is important / provides information about who I should spend time with.

"I wasn't mad at you. Like, you didn't do anything but be great. I guess I was jealous? I don't know. I was mad that you didn't tell me," she says. "Anyway, the chick I talked to said that the special is happening tomorrow. Brace yourself. Could be more news vans."

"Yeah."

"My mom wants to know if you want us to record it for you," she says.

"No thanks. I'm good."

We hang up. I ask Daddy to get paint at the hardware store so we can repaint the walls once we find them.

"I want candy," Mama says. "I need sugar."

"I will get your favorites," Daddy says / kisses her sweetly on the cheek.

Everything seems so normal / we still live in a series of half-broken plywood boxes / nothing is normal.

The minute Carmichael and Daddy leave the driveway in Carmichael's pickup truck, I decide to collapse the house on my own / stop time and leave Mama and Richard frozen where they stand / start pulling nails.

When I look out to the street, I can see Carmichael's pickup truck frozen at the first stop sign / Carmichael frozen at the wheel / and Daddy / and Daddy walking back to the house.

Tiny Bombs

ARGUMENT

I have never seen Daddy angry. Even when my sister still lived here and accused him of every torture he never did, he stayed level. As he walks toward the house, he looks furious.

I can't decide whether to start time again or not. Mama's still frozen working in the foyer / Richard is frozen somewhere in the hallway between box #11 and his bathroom.

I take my crowbar to the plywood near the switch / rip out as many nails as I can / he walks in / takes the crowbar from me. For a split second, I think he might hit me / he hugs me instead.

"You cannot just do this trick," he says.

"You do it all the time," I say.

"It is different for me," he says.

"How?"

"I—I am man and you are girl and it can hurt you."

I give him a look like his brain has turned to processed food / pathetic.

"Your brother and mother will be harmed."

"Fine," I say / start time again / zing!

"Back already?" Mama asks Daddy / looking for Skittles / Reese's Peanut Butter Cups.

Daddy says, "Just forgot a thing. Will be back soon!"

When he leaves, Mama says her hands feel weird. "Like pins and needles. I'm going to sit down for a little."

I go to Richard. He's ripping nails out / an anger machine in the southwest corridor. I start ripping nails out right next to him. We get a single eight-by-four sheet of plywood down / expose a section of tiny bombs.

"I'll go flip the main box switch. We can rip that conduit out and go from there," I say.

"Let's get the other wall first. Daddy can figure out the wires. He's the one who rerouted them all."

We work on the next wall, and the next, until box #11 is nearly collapsed.

"Something's holding them all together. I can't figure it out," Richard says.

We move to the foyer. Mama is back up on a chair, pulling nails gently and slowly. Richard tells her to go sit outside for a while / get fresh air / we rip apart box #1 / the foyer / find the pretty wallpaper underneath the plywood.

My room. Because it was next to her room, was more fully boxed. I want to see my carpet again / I start on the floor pieces. Richard starts in the hallway where the bulk of the building was done to keep me safe.

"Tru," he calls / nearly whispers. I step out of my room / he points to the wall he's just disassembled. It's covered in tiny bombs / a million tiny bombs / a billion tiny bombs.

We move toward her room / box #9 and it's still gone.

"What the fuck?" Richard says.

"I collapsed it last night," I say, "from the basement side."

"How can there be nothing here, and from the outside, the house looks fine?"

I shrug because I really don't know / too many questions / this explanation will do.

I stop time again / Richard freezes / Daddy should be mid–hardware store / no time to run home.

I take out every last nail around the whole east side of the house. I do the same to the west side / I don't even count nails / the whole place is ready to collapse / still bound by Daddy's secret conduit / to understand anything is to understand energy. I start time again / Richard looks at me and says, "That's weird. I can't feel my feet."

"Go out with Mama and get some rest. Drink water," I say.

US

It's just me and the switch / staring at each other.

> x equals me knowing what the switch is.
> x equals not knowing what to do about it.

Here's my dilemma / Psych Team / 60 Minutes / little Jennifer in Nebraska who can fly / I may never throw a javelin / myself / again. Religions could be built around the existence of this switch / every person in the world would want to own it / the government must never know.

When Richard comes back in, he starts moving plywood panels to the backyard. Mama stops me in the kitchen and looks in my eyes / sees all of it / looks toward the switch.

"Truda."

"Yes."

"When did time stop?"

"June twenty-third, 2020," I say.

"And when did I move out?"

"June twentieth," I say.

"And when did he leave his job?"

"Two days later—the twenty-second."

She nods / walks back outside / sits in her front yard / Miami chair.

I stare at the box / am sad I will stop a little girl from flying.

CARMICHAEL'S FAST-FOOD DINNER MENU

Carmichael and Daddy arrive home with fast-food dinner.

"Everyone gets chicken sandwich," Daddy says. "It was only logical choice."

No one complains / we eat chicken sandwiches / French fries.

Daddy says, "You have taken boxes down."

"Most of them," Richard says.

"We need your help with the wires," I say.

"And the bombs," Daddy says. He looks at his Wendy's chicken sandwich / hands it to Carmichael / stands up.

"And the bombs," Richard says.

BAYONET

Richard / rifle / cannot stab ideas / Mama hands him a bayonet.

"It's time to start over," she says.

"You can't just start over," Richard argues.

"You can," Mama says, "if you want to. You can do anything you want to. Anything."

Richard chews on this along with his chicken sandwich.

"You start by letting go of your mistakes," Mama says.

A.S. King

x equals Joy / Trust / Fear / Surprise / Sadness / Disgust / Anger
/ Anticipation.
x equals everything you ever felt / believed / heard could be a lie.
x equals stab that shit / those lies / with a bayonet.

REASSEMBLY INSTRUCTIONS NOT ENCLOSED

Richard says it's six o'clock N3WCLOCK time. We get back to work.

Mama handles the tiny bombs / land mines in the walls / expert detector / puts them in a hippie sling-bag she's wrapped around her body. I follow behind her, freeing conduit and wire as we go.

Daddy and Carmichael trace rerouted wires and disconnect them / back to precision energy / boring but efficient / the idea is to change the world *outside* your house / when you come home the little men in the wall sockets will say "Ooo!" / your water heater will work / will not be in the backyard.

Richard starts to patch holes in walls and ceilings / is in deep thought / letting go of his mistakes / coming to terms with the danger he once believed he was in.

Carmichael begins to rebuild bathrooms / replaces my broken shower door / gets one toilet working / collects the full bathroom buckets from the backyard / flushes / flushes / flushes.

Mama and I move the last plywood pieces out to the yard / she finds the vacuum cleaner / I look forward to sitting on my carpet again / maybe going to the podiatrist one day about the splinter.

We work into the night / putting things right—small things. Beds / chairs / sofas / dust / ballpoint pens in a mug / we paint over sanded spackle and replace fixings for the window blinds.

Richard asks, as Mama and I move through the house replacing light bulbs, "Are we even going to sleep tonight? It's two in the morning!"

I say, "Let's just finish and call it an all-nighter. Worth it."

Richard still looks wary.

"What's wrong?" I ask.

ON / OFF

On off on off on
Off on off on off.
Richard is crying again
and the moon is
extra big tonight—

On off on off on off on off.

When you look at
a light switch upside down,
when it's on,
it reads NO.

I think Richard's light switch
is upside down.

GHOST

Mama and I hug him. I take the right side; she takes the left.

"Is it really over?" he asks.

"That's up to you," she says.

"It's really over," I say. "And you didn't deserve any of it."

Daddy walks in and wraps his arms around all of us. Carmichael

left an hour ago / we have working plumbing again / he kissed me
on the cheek and told me to beat my own world record this week.

"It's so vague," Richard sobs. "We all know what the problem
is. Why don't we just talk about it? About her?"

The terror in all of our eyes right now would make you hide in
your closet / we are about to pull off a bank heist / roped you into
being the getaway driver. The room goes quiet. Sister is like carbon
monoxide / seeps through the floorboards / you never wake up.

Richard and I knew deep down. To understand anything is to
understand energy / bad energy is important, too.

It hits you at the most important times / all the times / all
times are important. All times are important until they aren't anymore. Take away time / life without time / own the arrow / it is
yours / you can fly.

N3WCLOCK 5:00 A.M.

We are purging / already purged the sister / took one hour / easy work / lies disintegrate when shared / we have moved now to regrets.

Mama says, "I'm so sorry for all the pain I caused when I didn't come home. I meant to," she says. "I really meant to come home. But she would tell me that you all were so happy I'd gone. She told me I'd be better off dead than by myself. I nearly did it. Nearly." She cracks / is suddenly sobbing. Richard moves from his spot on the sofa / stands next to her / rubs her back.

Daddy says, "It is shameful that my family is broken. I have not listened."

Mama keeps sobbing / catches her breath. "Honey, I left you for no reason. Isn't that awful? I mean, sure, you were a pain in the ass with all this weird safety stuff, but you always loved me. You all did. And it's so hard to believe!" She bends into a sob again. Richard rubs her back.

"Do you know what I want to know?" Richard says. "I want to know what to do now."

EXTERMINATOR

There are no exterminators for some things. No medication. No doctors or cures. No vaccines. There are no police for some things. No jail. No probation or community service. Some things are ghosts / insects in the brain. Some things have to die in their own time.

I say, "We have insects in our brains."

I am in the arrow. Everyone is frozen in their answer to this / there is no answer to this.

FLIPPING PANCAKES

I say to all of them, in answer to Richard's question, "You used to tell me that changing my mind was like flipping pancakes. Let's use this meeting to flip our pancakes. Heal, you know?"

"Heal? You're sixteen. How do you even know about healing?" Richard says.

"Your sister reads psychology, son. You forget project," Daddy says.

"We need to heal a lot," I say. "And Daddy will come to therapy with us. We'll go as a family."

"How do we explain it?" Richard asks.

"We tell our stories. That's it."

"It will hurt," Mama says. "And it won't be instant." She looks at me / I know why.

We sit in silence and breathe.

I look at Richard. "I miss you even though I've lived with you my whole life, and I don't think I really know you," I say.

Richard nods. "Me too."

In my head, there is a switch. It controls the past and the future / negative / positive. It can't control the present, but the present is always moving / in the arrow / which is fine because it only takes a second to make it into past.

WHAT TO DO WITH YOUR PAST

Serve it with lemons and curdled milk
with shortbread biscuits
make the day gray
spots of rain.

Make a quilt out of the villains
crochet the heroes together in a hat
Wear the hat. Use the quilt
as a picnic blanket.

Bring your friends.
Watch the squirrels be tiny monkeys
dare-deviling the trees.
Exclaim things!

Each lemon, sup of tea, cookie
is a bite into the future /
will digest, exit, and swim.
Digest. Exit. Swim.

Drink the curdled milk and get sick
watch your friends clean up
hold your hair back / hat on
hand you a tissue.

When you wash the vomit
out of the villainous quilt
each time it gets weaker.
Picnic often.

Richard and Mama go to bed while Daddy and I keep working on the kitchen. His goal is to get the cabinets up by dawn / we both know it's too close to dawn to succeed. We are a dilemma / a solution standing in a bare-bulb-lit kitchen / we know what to do.

"We can't," he says.

"We can," I say. "Brunch right here tomorrow seems like a good start to a new life."

It's a standoff / neither of us wants to show the other that we have power.

Finally, I do it. He gives me a mixed look—concern and pride / says every father to every powerful daughter / no cheap American high school hors d'oeuvre / no fancy toothpick. He is predictably Somewhere Else / protective of daughters / The Man of the House. I'm fine with it / have needed protection / will need it until the insects are all-the-way gone.

PLUTCHIK'S SUNDAY POTLUCK BRUNCH

Richard brings Surprise. "How did you get this done in three hours?" he asks us.

Mama brings Joy. "Look at it! It's like nothing ever happened," she says.

Daddy brings Anticipation. "We are new family now. So many things will we do!"

I bring Trust / smile a lot / don't say much / love every one of these people not because they are family / because they love me / because they allowed me to fly.

We are in the kitchen / in the arrow in the kitchen / Daddy

and I didn't count the hours it took, but I'd guess it was six hours by the time we got the countertops reinstalled / caulked in / under cabinet lights working. We didn't talk at all / communication in time is different / psychic / Mama probably dreamed it all as she slept.

"I want one last family meeting today," Mama says.

Richard and I both groan. That's five / too many / one week.

Daddy says, "Will be short. We will talk quickly."

"I have to go to Carrie's to—uh—work on a paper that's due tomorrow."

"You're a terrible liar," Mama says.

"I don't want to miss your show," Richard says.

"It's not my show. I didn't even talk to them."

"What show?" Mama asks.

"60 Minutes!" Richard says.

I smile at Richard / say nothing / it takes him a moment.

"Oh, snap," he says. "Busted."

I say, "They wanted me to talk about being a time anomaly. I don't think I am one."

Daddy says, "You are very talented girl."

"Exactly," Mama says.

"I still think we should watch it," Richard says.

"Carrie's mom is recording it for you," I say.

Daddy serves a perfect eggs Benedict. He makes mimosas for him and Mama / squeezed oranges first thing this morning. We eat / four dinner chairs / four plates / a family / in the arrow.

I eye the switch with every bite / chew it like bubble gum / am ready to blow the bubble.

FAMILY MEETING #543

To understand anything is to understand energy. Mama is in her chair / Daddy on the couch, lying with his feet up / Richard is in his beanbag / I sprawl on the love seat.

"I'll call this to order," Mama says. "Talk to me about life, you two. What are you working on? What's happening this week? Can I help with anything?"

I wait for Richard to go first. As he talks, I see Daddy's eyes closing involuntarily / we destroyed and rebuilt an entire house / family / in a day / he is tired. Richard doesn't see this from the beanbag / keeps talking. Coding class / calculus / ecology / online classes are harder / but.

"I'm excited to write the analysis paper for my lit class. I started writing it a few weeks ago but I have to start over."

"*Lolita?*" I ask.

"I changed my mind," he says / idea-stabber / mind-changer. "I was only reading it again to make sure I wasn't—you know—like him."

"Oh, honey," Mama says. "You aren't like that. I told you. The bad energy just got into your head."

"I feel so stupid," he says.

"We all feel stupid," Mama says.

"What do you feel stupid about?" he asks.

Mama says. "I abandoned my family!"

"We thought you were a yo-yo," I say.

"I *was* a yo-yo!" she says and laughs. "I'm a fucking clairvoyant. And I still let it happen. I'll feel dumb for that for a long time." She looks at Richard. "We'll work it out."

Richard seems to believe it / looks ready for a dare.

I watch Daddy's eyelids.

"I have to have a thesis statement written by tomorrow for our Solution Time project," I say.

"Sounds easy," Mama says.

I look at the switch.

Richard says, "She's been trying to write it for five months."

"Shit," Mama says. "Can we help you?"

I breathe / Daddy's eyelids are dancing. "I'll figure it out."

"Well, what's it about?" Mama asks.

"People giving a shit about other people," I answer.

"Like—all people?" she asks.

"It's too wide. That's why I can't get the thesis statement down."

"Wasn't that class supposed to have something to do with time?" she asks.

"I studied the psychology of time. And I argued that time stopped because it was sick of us being assholes to each other. So the only way to start it again is to stop being assholes to each other."

"Good luck," Mama says.

"Yeah," I say / I get up / walk to the kitchen / to the tool bucket / get my crowbar and Daddy's claw hammer.

I say, "Technically, it's not due tomorrow."

Freeze. Nobody make a fucking move.

I start with my crowbar / use both hands.

THE ORIGINAL BOX

There are layers here / slide the hook between them / pull. Whole boxes come off, one at a time. One is made of old paneling. One is made of old vegetable crates. One is made of white pressboard. One is made of my father's old skateboards. In between there is plywood / oak / maple / cherry / ash / teak / mahogany / sticks and nests / birds / eggshells / saplings / peach buds / there is sky. I remove layer after layer in near silence. Everyone in the living room is frozen, but Daddy is only sleeping.

Finally, I reach the original box.

I use Daddy's hammer to carefully remove it and expose the switch.

Like flipping pancakes.

THE SWITCH III

To understand anything is to understand energy. In the arrow, energy doesn't stop / I am in the arrow / am the arrow / the arrow is me. Zeno wasn't wrong / time stands still every single day. Entire nations are stuck in arrows. Entire families. Entire classrooms. Entire galaxies—flying through time inside an unmoving arrow.

Everything is wrong with the world / people had nine months to stop being assholes to one another / they didn't stop.

x equals they didn't stop.

In the center of our house, there is a switch. I know what the switch controls.

"Don't touch it!" Daddy yells / starts time again.

Because Daddy is lunging toward me, Richard / reanimated / lunges for me, too.

Mama sits calmly, inspecting the pins and needles in her hands.
I decide for the world / for the flying girl / for me.
I flip the switch.

Nothing explodes / erupts / nothing eerie happens. Just the clock
on the oven starts blinking. The analog on the wall—Daddy hung
it last night on the same nail—starts to tick.

Mama looks at her watch / Daddy and Richard stop running
toward me.

I take my phone out of my pocket.

Date: March 28, 2021 / Time: 5:48 p.m.

Richard / rifle with a new bayonet looks around the house as
if he just landed here / knows us all through a dream. There are
no more bombs.

Daddy stares at me angry / in love. To understand anything is
to understand energy / anger / love.

x equals anger.

x equals love.

Flip the pancake / take the tampões de ouvido out of your ears
/ hear everything / listen.

OLDCLOCK

N3WCLOCK stock tanked first thing Monday morning. They lost
everything / news mocked them by noon / dumb kids who
couldn't get into a better college. Things went back to normal /

people were bigger assholes to one another / by dinnertime, approximately four billion were scolded for being late to the table.

Scientists had spent Sunday night doing mathematical time equations to make sure we had the time right / headlines increased the font size / **279** / that's how many days / nine months + six days = **279**. Graphic designers had logos ready / by lunchtime at the home of the Trojans there were more than three hundred t-shirt styles available in the "279" store.

No one would ever know how Daddy did it. Even he couldn't explain it when we asked. "My intent was to save electric money," he said. "Was inventing for water heater." Mama reckoned he was desperate / to understand anything is to understand energy / his sadness needed time to reorient / he bought time / with Somewhere Else ingenuity / not a billion dollars.

We didn't move it / dare touch it after I'd flipped it. The four of us built a box / together / agreed we would never touch it again / or only in case of emergencies / Mama made us pinky-swear / embarrassed Daddy into pinky-swearing, too.

Solution Time was cancelled / of course it was / Nigel is not in school today. Rumor has it he was moved to another position / administration / waste of his transformational wit / writing letters to school families about spirit days / yearbooks / sandwich sales.

Psych Team still meets in our usual classroom / we do Anticipation for fun / last stop on the last cycle around Plutchik's Clock. I write phrases and words on the whiteboard / habit / healing. *Curious, inquisitive, excited! Interested and engaged—willing to wait because you know what's coming is good. Giddy, nervous, edgy with waiting, awake and paying* attention, the feeling of want and the fear of it not being as great as you thought. Relief from other emotions, a way up and a way out. Preparing and planning. Like the night before your birthday. Feeling like tomorrow is going to be good. Dreams. Hopes. The future. I take a picture of it for my notes, even though my notes are moot / Solution Time is over / I have no control over people giving a shit about other people / only myself.

At lunch, while half the cafeteria buys "279" T-shirts, Len shows me a news story on his phone. Puts both earbuds in my ears / takes reaction video / it's little Jennifer from Omaha, flying around the field behind her house / breaking news.

Breaking news / I'm at track practice. Breaking news / tomorrow is our first away meet. Breaking news / I finally found something I'm good at in high school.

Breaking news / you are the energy.
Breaking news / here is a switch.

Acknowledgments

Reader, when I was eighteen, I got so tired of being hyper-aware of / scared of / concerned with time that I took my watch off my wrist, threw it into a public trash can, and never put one on again. More than thirty years later, I have to say, it was one of the best things I ever did for myself. After that, I grew my own time / did things that made people wonder about me, like volunteering, giving up TV, living off the land, and writing weird novels—things I *wanted* to do.

Class of 2020, I dedicate this book to you because you graduated during a time that tossed its watch into a public trash can. You can now grow your own time, too. Take the dare. Be extraordinary. Live the heck out of your life. Drop me a line and tell me what you're up to.

I owe thanks to all the usual suspects. Everyone at Dutton Books for Young Readers, but especially my editor, Andrew Karre. Special shout-out to Samira Iravani and Nicki Crock for this amazing cover and Anne Heausler for making me be a better person.

Thank you to Michael Bourret for being an epic human being and a great agent.

Thank you to my friends, many of them writers, but many who are not and yet they work to understand my bizarro life. You all know who you are and I love you.

Thank you to teachers and librarians and bloggers and booksellers who share my books with readers. Thank you to fans who write me letters that keep me going. Thank you to Livy King, who is so rad, I can't believe I'm this lucky—I love you. Thank you to Gracie King for giving me sixteen years with her wild mind and beautiful heart—I miss you. Thank you to my parents who have supported me since the beginning—from taking me to meet Grace Hopper to mass-photocopying my first typewritten newspaper in 1982—you two have always understood that I have something to say.

I owe special thanks to the crew at the Johnson County Library system for asking me to write a speech about time in 2018. That's where I invented Plutchik's Clock. It was like throwing my watch into a trash can again / reminded me what's important.

To anyone who needs to hear it: Time means nothing. Money means very little. Love means everything. Build a Plutchik's Clock. Find your switch / pull your switch / soar.